Four helicopters had landed. Two were full and beginning to take off when one of the huge men slammed his fist into the side of the tail section creating a huge hole. The chopper tried to take off but the man amazingly held it down. The craft swayed from side to side until its spinning blades touched the ground drawing it on its side. The helicopter burst into flames seconds later exploding into a shower of fragged metal.

From the fiery blaze Max watched the huge man walk towards him. He was on fire and sections of his skin had burned off. From where Max stood he thought he saw the blinking of diodes and the flashing of circuitry.

The man drew near Max its red eyes glowing in the early morning darkness. Max raised his rifle and fired the whole clip off into the man. His forward progress didn't falter. The man was close enough for Max to get a good look. The flesh had burned away leaving a dull gray but clearly distinguishable metal plating. Its red diode like eyes showing no emotion only a clear determination to kill him.

The
Time
Dominators

By
Antonio Collado

A Time Work Book

THE TIME DOMINATORS

Copyright 1991 by Antonio Collado

This book may not be reproduced in whole or in
part without consent from the author.
For information address: Time Work Books,
co/Antonio Collado, Bx 421, Rockland ME.
04841

Published by Time Work Books

First printing, April 1992

ISBN: 0-9632826-0-3

Library of Congress Catalog Card
Number: 91-91461

Printed in the United States of America

COVER ART by JOHN A COLLADO

For Mom
Who's time had slipped
Through the hourglass
Like grains of Sand

CONTENTS

1   Beginning
2   Reanimation
3   Impact
4   Auto Destruct
5   Night Fight
6   Past Tense
7   Ensnared
8   Foresight
9   Susan
10 Deaths Forgiveness
11 Build Up
12 Deceived
13 Calm Before the Storm
14 Into Tomorrow
15 WAR!
16 Mirage
17 Then There Were Three
18 Phoenix
19 End Game
    Epilogue

The Time Dominators

From around the turn the horses raced,
their jockeys flailing them with their crops
trying to get a feeble amount of lead. Their
thundering hooves could barely be heard over
the roaring crowd. In front was Whispering
Song followed closely by Venus Fire. They
were sure winners and a few safe betters
placed a small bet knowing full well it would
pay off. The horses rounded the final turn
heading for the finish line. Over the excited
crowd the announcer could be heard calling off
each horse in the order of its lead. From out
of the rear came Midnight Express the horse
that had the greatest odds. To many people it
was a sure loser and didn't warrant wasting
their hard earned cash. But for one man the
horse was a guaranteed fortune. Max Storm sat
back in his chair, he didn't need to watch for
he already knew the outcome of the race. A
hush came over the crowd as Midnight Express
took the lead and crossed the finish line a
full length ahead of the rest. Most peoples'
dreams shattered that day, fortunes lost lives
ruined. All except for one man, who had moved
from the swelling crowd to claim his fortune.
The fire crackled and popped, from a
comfortable high back chair Max Storm stared
at the newspapers headline. "Largest Bet Pays
Off!" The story told of how a man nobody
knew, came and placed an extremely large bet
on a sure loser and walked away a millionaire.
He sipped his brandy and chuckled to himself.
"If only people knew the truth," He
thought to himself.
"If only everybody on the planet had known
how close to death they had come."
Max rose and walked over to the small

bar that sat against the far wall refilling
his brandy snifter. Turning he looked around
the room, the light from the fire creating
eerie shadows that danced over all the books
lining the walls. The door handle turned on
one of the french doors and slowly opened. In
walked a man of seventy his face very wrinkled
and what was left of his gray hair combed back
on both sides. He was dressed in a suit and
bow tie and a pair of very shiny black oxford
shoes.

"Good evening Max. I just came to tell
you that Martha and I will be going out this
evening. We just didn't want you to worry if
you found us gone. After what happened
before . . . well . . . ."

"Yes, your right James. We can't let down
our guard, not ever again," Max stared into
the burning fire.

"Have a good time James, where are you
going?"

"Martha had her heart set on seeing the
Russian ballet. I personally can't stand to
watch it but . . . , Why don't you ask Susan
and join us?"

"No, that's all right. This is one
evening
I really need to be alone. Just a good book,
a warm fire and myself. Thank you though."

James nodded and headed for the door. He
hesitated before opening it.

"You know Max, you have been through a very
rough time. You can't blame yourself for what
happened. You did what you had to do. It's
over for now and you have to try and find some
peace within yourself. Have a good evening
Max."

The door closed behind him leaving Max

alone again with the dancing shadows. He'd
known James all his life, James had been his
fathers butler and for all Max could remember
he had been more of a father than his own. He
trusted his judgment and he knew he had to
come to terms with what had happened and the
position he now held. He placed himself back
into the chair and picked up the newspaper
staring at his faded picture on the front
page.

So much had happened in nine months. His
eye's stared into the fire and his mind
drifted.

CHAPTER ONE

Beginning

Max Storm was five as he clung tightly
to the door of his parents '57 Buick. The
tires squealed as the car swung around the
sharp curves of Breakman Ridge. New Hampshire
was scenic country and Max enjoyed the Sundays
his family went on picnics. Today he was
terrified. They were halfway up the
Kangamangus Highway when they came upon a
stalled car with the hood up. Max sensed
something wrong as his father screeched the
car to a halt and jumped out.
   "Stay here, I have to warn them," His
father spoke calmly.
Max watched his father move toward the open
hood. He was about to ask his mother Virginia
what his father was going to warn them about.
Before he could utter the words he watched his
father recoil and race back to their car the
fear and shock evident on his face.
His father jammed the car into gear and sped
off down the road. Max saw his fathers hands
tremble at the steering wheel. He was
oblivious to everything except the road that

twisted in front of him. A chill ran through Max, his father was very rational not driven easily to hysterics.

"Sam! What is it? What did you see back there?" Virginia looked shakily at her husband.

His father ignored his mothers question and kept on driving as if the devil himself was behind him. Rounding a curve Sam reacted to slowly. Directly in front of them was a large tree sprawled across the road. He slammed hard on the brakes but it was too late. The car struck the tree crushing in the front end and sending the drivers side broadside. Max was thrown over the front seat toward the solid steel dash. Virginia Storm reacted quickly putting herself in front of her son. The impact of Max's body and her own against the dash bruised her ribs. Sam collided against the steering wheel his head hitting the roof and sending him into darkness.

Max awoke to the sound of his mother screaming. His eyes opened to see a huge man standing outside his fathers door. His hand burst through the side window and grabbed the door ripping it clear from the car. The man reached inside and grabbed Max's father pulling him out and laying him along side of the car. He then reached in and grabbed a screaming Virginia by the hair dragging her out. Max was terrified, even at five he understood that somebody was hurting his parents. He had to help somehow. He opened the door and raced around to where his mother was drawn out. The man had her firmly around the throat her feet dangling off the ground. Max jumped as high as he could to grab the man around the neck. The man dropped Virginia and turned to face his new opponent. Max never even saw it coming. A quick glint of steel flashed in the man's hand then across Max's face. Max fell off hitting the ground screaming. Virginia despite her pain was onto the man.

"Maxwell run! Run into the woods! Run," She screamed as she tried to direct the man's attention away from her son. Max still holding onto his bloodied face stood up and ran disappearing over the steep embankment.

The man's attention now focused onto Virginia. Max peered through the tall grass that grew along the embankment. The man grabbed his mother by the throat again. Max caught something moving from behind the car. Another man appeared dressed in almost all black and moved quickly up behind the tall man. Max watched as the second man pulled a gun out placing it directly against the tall mans head. Max felt strange and darkness quickly surrounded him. He felt himself slipping down the embankment as he heard the shot echo, then darkness.

Max next awoke screaming in a hospital. He learned later that he was found wandering aimlessly down the road. A large gash extending from just below his eye to the bottom of his jaw. Nobody had heard from or seen his parents again. It was determined by the police that his parents were murdered. Max had given them as best of a description of the man as he could remember. He was placed in the care of his parents house-keepers, James and Martha. They were always like grandparents to him and now they

had become his surrogate parents. Life
resumed it's almost normal routine. Every so
often Max was brought down to the Police
station in an attempt to identify the
attacker. In each case Max failed to identify
the tall man who had killed his parents.
Eventually the case was placed in with the
many other unsolved files.

When Max turned eighteen the courts
awarded him what was left of the Storm estate.
He had inherited his fathers Bioelectronic
industry "GeneticBoard Ind." The years
away without good decisive management had
taken its toll and Max was forced to sell it.
He was able to keep his father's mansion that
was located at the top of Cynet Mountain. The
life insurance policies paid off handsomely
allowing him to pay most of the other failed
business debts. Not long after Max was
deciding weather or not to go to college. He
didn't have much time the draft had caught up
with him. The Vietnam war was in its seventh
year. He could have gotten himself out of it
but he was feeling restless and tied down and
the army was his ticket out for something
different. He made James and Martha legal
overseers of his estate, packed his bags and
left. Army life appealed to him and he
advanced quickly becoming a Green Beret and
learning everything from stealth assaults to
flying helicopters. He had seen three tours
in the bush and he enjoyed going out on
reconnaissance missions. Every time the high
ranking brass tried to tie him down to a desk
job he managed to pull the right strings to
keep himself in combat.

Max survived the bloodiest of encounters

and always came back with the most kills and
the fewest casualties. He was quickly
promoted to Lieutenant and drew the largest
company of men. They believed in him and his
abilities.

In 1973 the war was slowly drawing to a
close. Max was given orders to infiltrate
what intelligence had found to be a POW camp
to the north. They flew in under the cover of
darkness and met stiff opposition upon
entering the camp. They found the POW's, ten
of them in pretty rough shape. They had left
the camp a wasteland and headed as quickly as
possible back to the LZ. for their pickup. When
they reached the LZ. they came under fire. The
Viet Cong were positioned near the tree line
and dug in deeply. Mortar shells exploded all
around them and bullets zinged through the
dense underbrush. One by one Max's men began
to fall. They were being slowly annihilated
with no where to go until the choppers came.

In the distance the thumping sounds of
rotor blades echoed. It was almost dawn when
the dark silhouette of the helicopters came
into view. Max and his men broke from the
tree line. Tracer bullets flew all around them
striking each of his men with a deadly
accuracy. Charlie had no plans to let them
escape, they broke from their positions
to intercept the retreating GI's. Max watched
them emerge from the jungle. They were
dressed like Viet Cong only they were huge
with broad massive forms. Fear gripped Max
Storm a fear he hadn't known since his youth.
His men fired point blank at them the cloth on

their uniforms ripping but failing to slow
them down. The fear grew within him and he
ordered his men into the choppers and not to
stand and fight.
   Four helicopters had landed. Two were full
and beginning to take off when one huge men
slammed his fist into the side of the tail
section creating a huge hole. The chopper
tried to take off but the man amazingly held
it down. The craft swayed from side to side
until its spinning blades touched the ground
drawing it on its side. The helicopter burst
into flames seconds later exploding into a
shower of fragged metal.
      From the fiery blaze Max watched the
huge man walk toward him. He was on fire and
sections of his skin had burned off. From
where Max stood he thought he saw the blinking
of diodes and the flashing of circuitry.
   The man drew near Max its red eyes glowing
in the early morning darkness. Max raised his
rifle and fired the whole clip off into the
man. His forward progress didn't falter. The
man was close enough for Max to get a good
look. The flesh had burned away leaving a
dull gray but clearly distinguishable
metal plating. Its red diode like eyes
showing no emotion only a clear
determination to kill him. Max struck his
enemy in the head using his gun as a club.
The stock broke but the head didn't even
flinch. Its hand struck out hitting the side
of Max's helmet. The impact sent Max
sprawling. The thing lumbered over him moving
in for the kill. Max pulled the pin on a
grenade and shoved it into what was left of
its tattered clothing. He pushed himself as

close to the ground as possible. He could
feel the force of the explosion. Hot
fragments of metal showered over him. A
couple embedding themselves into is right leg
and back. The pain was excruciating and he
fought to keep conscious.

He suddenly felt the firm hands of somebody
picking him up and dragging him to a chopper.
He was aware of the bullets and mortars
zinging and exploding around him.

"Hold onto that rope there LT., yer safe
now," The familiar voice of his best friend
Tinker called to him.

They had been together since boot camp and
had become as close to brothers as they
could get. Tinker refused his own command to
stay with Max. Tinker helped another man into
the helicopter and was climbing in himself
when a mortar exploded underneath him. It all
happened in slow motion. Max watched the
flash form under Tinker, then his legs seemed
to fly off into different directions. Max
screamed and lunged out grabbing hold of
Tinkers suspenders. The chopper lifted up off
the ground and Max watched the carnage filled
patty below him. Two of the four helicopters
had made it. Below Max could see what was
left of his men being butchered by the metal
things that attacked them, he could even see
what was left of the one he exploded crawling
around still looking for something to kill.

Tinker lived just barely but his life
would never be the same. Max had resigned the
same time. The rest of his men blamed him
for what had happened. He had lost their
trust and knew he had reached the end of his
military career.

CHAPTER TWO

Reanimation

Max came home to a wonderful homecoming set up by James and Martha. There was a small gathering of Max's highschool buddies. They seemed no different than when he left. They also expected him to be no different as if the war had been one big joke. But he was different, he had changed greatly since entering the service. His outlook on life had changed. His last mission had done that. He felt terribly worried, he had witnessed something that was not natural or normal and he somehow was a key player with the world as a prize.

Max smiled and played his part. These people he knew were no longer a part of his world. The war had made them a memory. The evening quickly ended and he was left alone in the huge kitchen with James and Martha. The silence was eerie and James finally cut it.

"Max my boy its good to have to back. But I feel that there's something bothering you."

"I feel it also Maxwell. I've known you since you were born and I know when something isn't right," Martha cut in.

"It's the war . . . it's . . . I don't know! I need to know more about my parents, my background. What exactly was my father's

-11-

business about? What was my father working on
when he and mom disappeared? And for that
matter are they dead or alive someplace being
held all these years by some corrupt country?"

Max took a sip of his coffee and stared
into space. James led Martha out of the
kitchen.

"I will talk to him, he must know the
truth. All I hope is that he doesn't hate us
for it."

Martha nodded and headed up the stairs. She
hesitated and looked James in the eyes. She
didn't envy him for what he had to do now.
James nodded back and pushed through the
polished swinging doors that led to the
kitchen. Max still sat drinking his coffee.
James poured himself a cup and sat down in
front of him.

"Max, you must understand that what I'm
about to tell you I kept from you for your own
good. Your father was a brilliant man. Most
of the militaries computer technology came
from him. That is how your father earned his
fortune. He was a very kind person, he
treated his employees well and was a very good
father for the years you were together. A lot
of him is in you. The way you act the
kindness you bear, the quick thinking that
made you and your men survive the war. Your
father was all this and more.

One day your father and his best friend and
top scientist were working with an electron
accelerator. Experimenting with electro-
magnets and the effects huge amounts of
electricity had on the electron. In doing so
the electron disappeared and reappeared ten
minutes later."

"What was he trying to succeed at?" Max

asked listening intently on every word James
spoke.

"You must realized that this was at the
height of the second world war. The country
needed something to make its planes and ships
invisible to enemy radar. By our third year
into the war your father had constructed a
device run by a turbine using huge semi-
conductors to channel vast amounts of
electricity. The idea was to blanket the ship
with these electron rays rendering it
invisible to radar. The experiment started
off well and succeeded in making the ship
invisible but something went wrong. The ship
completely disappeared. It appeared two hours
later off the coast of Virginia. Half the
crew was missing the others were cut up and
mauled."

"Where there any survivors?" Max asked
becoming more interested every minute.

"Yes there were survivors. They were
declared insane and sent to institutions.
They babbled about a city with huge metal men
and machines everywhere. These metal men came
on board and began hauling them off and
slaughtering them all. The strange part of it
all is their stories were all the same. The
project was tagged a failure and your father
went back to the drawing board, only with a
very heavy conscious. People had died because
of something he created and it grieved him
deeply.

He listened intently to every sailor that
had been sent to asylums, the more he
listened the more he believed. The more he
questioned the more the military tried to shut
him up. He finally kept quiet and continued
on with his work. From all his findings he

concluded that the ship had traveled into future, how far he could only guess. He built a smaller power unit that he mounted into a large stainless steel pyramidal shaped machine."

"In short my father had created a time machine," Max spoke out astounded.

James nodded. "Your father was the first to try it. He went back into the seventeen hundreds. He had always wanted to meet George Washington. Well he found that the ship had transported him back there but he could only stay a very short while. The energy that the machine stored quickly dissipated. He found that he could only stay in a time period for a few short hours. He came back with trinkets for your mother and a gnawing urge to find a way to hold the energy for extended trips. He also felt uncomfortable with the fact that if something happened to him he would be alone and trapped. He wouldn't bring a companion, I know, I volunteered to go with him. He felt that he had caused enough pain with his experiments and that another life would never be taken due to his experiments.

Many years passed and he slowly changed. He became an obsessed man. He needed to find the answer to the energy problem and whenever he came close the answer seemed to elude him.

These were very dark years for Martha and I and even more so for your mother. They battled fiercely and your father turned to drinking. He almost left your mother when he learned that she was pregnant with you. Your birth changed a lot of things. Somehow it pulled your father out of the deep hole he had dug for himself. He became a man renewed.

He came to the conclusion that the answers

he searched for would only be found in the
future. Three weeks before your parents
disappeared he made his trip into the future.
The twentyfifth century to be as exact as I
can remember. He returned with the answers he
needed but also with a growing paranoia. He
kept mumbling that soon they would be here,
that the Annihilators were coming."

"Who are the Annihilators?" Max probed for
more information.

"I don't know Max. Your father closed up
to everyone soon after he returned. He always
looked over his shoulder from that day on.

Have you ever wondered why they never found
your parents? They only found the car and a
bunch of mechanical parts that were never
identified strewn on the ground. The police
threw out half of your statement because they
found it hard to believe. You had said a man
ripped the car door completely off its
hinges."

"Yes I did, I remember it all now. The man
did rip the door completely off."

"The police took it as an overactive
imagination along with the trauma of what you
went through," Max rose from the table.

"Where are you going?" James quickly
asked.

"I need to talk with one of the survivors
of that experiment."

"Max, there's more, please follow me."

James rose from the table leading Max down
the spiral stairs that led to the basement.
The downstairs was situated into four rooms
one of them being a study where his father did
all the paperwork. Another was a wine cellar.
The third just had storage inside. The fourth
and largest was his fathers workshop. He was

never allowed in there as a child and growing
up he never had the curiosity to see what lay
beyond the thick oak door that was locked and
bolted many times over. James led him to the
door and produced a key ring and began
unlocking the many locks. The door barely
moved and creaked from all its years of
stillness. James reached into the pitch black
room searching for the light switch.

Suddenly the room lit up, the walls were
lined with workbenches covered in mechanical
parts all heavily covered with dust. There
were racks with parts on them all labeled and
tagged. There were tape recorders and even a
computer that was advanced for its time. The
thing that caught Max's eye was the massive
form of something that was covered under an
old army tarp.

Max looked at James. "The time machine?" He
asked.

James walked over and began to draw the
tarp off, coughing and sneezing from the years
of dust that filled the room. Max helped him
and soon they stood before the massive
stainless steel hulk its metal still shiny.
The pyramid looked exact in measurement.
Where it came to a point at the top sat
a four foot high cylinder its metal black
compared to the stainless steel of the rest of
the machine.

"How do we get in?" Max asked excitedly.

James walked around the back of the machine
and pulled out a heavily insulated cord its
end forming five prongs that fit into a
special receptacle in the wall. Max watched
him slip the plug into the receptacle. There
instantly came a hissing sound and a flat
section of the machines wall began to open

forming a small ramp. The dark insides
instantly were lit up revealing three high
back leather bucket seats. In front of them
sat two television screens and one keyboard.
All around on the sides lights blinked on and
off the crudity of the small bulbs apparent.
   Max seemed fascinated with the blinking
lights. He slowly walked up the ramp entering
the machine. He felt the soft leather on the
headrest of the first chair. Excitement raced
through his veins, he actually had the power
to go through time!
   He sat down in the first chair and stared
at the computer console in front of him. He
also began to realize the awesome respons-
ibility that was now thrust into his life.
   James entered the machine and placed his
hand upon Max's shoulder.
   "IS HE ALL RIGHT JAMES? HIS PULSE AND
BLOOD PRESSURE ARE ABOVE NORMAL," A soft
gently soothing voice bounced off the metal of
the inner walls.
   Max leaped from the chair looking from side
to side.
   "Where did that come from?" He looked at
James and then out of the machine expecting to
see someone coming up the ramp.
   "I AM SAM STORMS TRAVELING COMPANION. MY
NAME IS SUSAN, I MONITOR ALL FUNCTIONS OF THE
TIME MACHINE. MY PRIMARY FUNCTION IS TO
ENSURE THE SAFETY AND RETURN OF MY CREATOR SAM
STORM. JAMES IT IS VERY GOOD TO SEE YOU, IT
HAS BEEN TOO LONG. SAM HAS NOT RETURNED IN
OVER FIFTEEN YEARS. WHO IS YOUR COMPANION?
WHERE IS SAM?"
   "Sam disappeared sixteen years ago Susan.
This is Maxwell Storm your creators son,"
There came a chilling silence.

"Susan were you very close to my father?"
Max asked.

"HE WAS MY CREATOR . . . MY FRIEND,"
Susan's voice sounded hurt.

"Susan, my father and mother disappeared
long ago not leaving any idea of where they
could have gone. Do you have any idea or
information in your data banks?" Max's voice
was tender yet stern.

"ON THE BASES OF DEDUCTION IT WOULD SEEM
THAT THE ANNIHILATORS HAVE SUCCEEDED IN
CATCHING UP WITH HIM."

"Who or what are the Annihilators?" Max
quickly shot back.

"THE ANNIHILATORS ARE . . . ;"

"Are What?" Max was becoming more
irritated.

"IT WOULD SEEM THAT EXTENSIVE PARTS OF MY
MEMORY BANKS HAVE BEEN ERASED. MY ONLY
RECOLLECTION WAS OF SOME BATTLE. YOUR FATHER
AND I BARELY ESCAPED WITH OUR . . . HIS LIFE.
THERE IS GREAT DANGER MAX STORM I CAN FEEL
IT."

Max grabbed James by the arm leading him
out of the machine.

"PLEASE COME BACK, DON'T LEAVE ME ALONE FOR
ANOTHER SIXTEEN YEARS. I WOULD RATHER BE SHUT
DOWN PERMANENTLY THAN REMAIN ALONE FOR SUCH A
LONG TIME."

"We will return Susan, I promise, you will
not be alone again," Max stared back at the
hulk of stainless steel still finding it hard
to believe.

"James, Susan is far more advanced than
this time period. Where did my father
get the technology to build her? She . . . ,
I mean it sounds as if IT has the ability to
feel emotion."

The Time Dominators

"I don't know where Susan came from or how your father managed to build her. I do know that she wasn't part of the machine before he went into the future. He had left that night in silence. Your mother didn't even know he had left until he returned. When he did Susan was there."

"Well it seems that someone or something didn't want any memory of that trip to ever be brought up again. I think we better start with finding out what were dealing with. Maybe some not so insane survivors can shed some light.

CHAPTER THREE

Impact

Max slipped the key into the ignition of the new yet old 69' GTO. He had bought it just before he went into the service. He and a few buddies at the time had overhauled the engine adding a small air inductor to give it that extra boost when he raced. He had big plans for the car. He had always wanted to race to become a professional driver maybe even drive in the Indy 500. Right now that was the furthest from his mind. He pumped the accelerator and adjusted the choke. The engine roared to life its deep throaty growl settling down into a pulsating purr.

He needed more information to try and piece the story together. He had gotten the information from his fathers study as to where each man was located. He wondered how many of them were still alive. Two were located in a New Hampshire institution in the White Mountains not far from where he lived.

He ran the car through its gears feeling the roughness of the Hurst shifter. The car ran just as good as the day he placed it into

the garage. The only indication of its
idleness was the layer of dust that covered
the shiny black of the body.

Max drove the car slowly down the steep
twisting road of Cynet Mountain. The view was
spectacular, awing him every time. He had
been to many lands but none he loved more than
the mountains of New Hampshire. The traffic
picked up when he reached the bottom of the
mountain. The road leading to Gorham was
usually busy. Max edged the car into the line
going into town. On the outskirts of town
heading on route 16 to North Conway Max
opened the car up. The speedometer jumped to
the seventy mark the engines growl increasing
a little.

Within a half hour he pulled the car into
the small parking lot of the Graham Station
Institution. There were few cars parked in
the lot. Max expected as much for a Sunday.
The sky had become overcast and looked as if
torrents of rain were about to come down. The
Institution was completely white on the
outside standing four stories high.
Max watched a silhouette walk by one of the
few windows. He shuddered to think of what
these men had been through, he had learned
that his father tried to gain their release
and that every attempt he made was thwarted
for some reason by the government.

He walked up to the reception desk to be
greeted by a rather burly woman in her
forties. Her hair was tied up in a bun giving
her the appearance of a strict school teacher.
Her dress was flowered and made her look twice
her size. Max expected a gruff voice but was
surprised when a very sweet and soft voice

reached his ears.

"Can I help you sir?" She looked up from her book.

"I was wondering if I could visit with two of your patients. One is a Norman Schruppt, the other is a Bob Fredricks."

"Are you a family member?" The burly woman quickly shot back.

"Not really, just a very close friend."

"Well, usually we don't allow visitors other than family members. I'll have to ask the head nurse for her approval."

The woman picked up her phone dialing some number inside the building. She spoke so softly that Max could only hear a few words. The burly woman looked up every now and then and smiled showing the space between her front teeth. Max rolled his eye's avoiding the womans flirting. The woman hung up the phone.

"The head nurse will be right out," She said smiling, Max smiled back.

A few moments later a buzzer could be heard and Max watched as a woman using a set of keys, opened and shut two doors walking up to the glass door that separated her from Max. She was a rather attractive woman. He would have placed her about twenty six. She had reddish brown hair with deep brown eyes that held authority. The shape of her curved body showed well beneath the tight nurses outfit. The door opened and Max came face to face with her.

"Hello, I understand that you wish to see two of our patients? Usually we only allow family to visit. What relationship do you have with them?"

The Time Dominators

"I actually have no relationship, I'm just
a friend. My father visited them regularly
quite a few years ago. Its very important
that I am allowed to speak with them."
"Well actually from what I understand a man
used to come and visit them. They haven't had
any visitors in the five years that I've been
here though, I guess it wouldn't hurt. Follow
me please."
She began unlocking the series of doors.
Max watched her hips sway and smiled to
himself. She led him to a small room with no
windows, a table and four chairs were the only
contents.
"Please wait here, I'll bring them in one
at a time."
Max pulled a chair out and sat down. He
needed to find out who the Annihilators were.
Somehow he felt that his last mission in Nam
was related.
The door opened and a frail man about forty
eight years old walked in. His face was
unshaven and his eyes were sunken.
"Bob, this is Mr. Storm. He wishes to
visit with you."
His eyes lit up at the sound of Max's last
name.
"Sam...?" The man squinted at Max.
"No, I'm his son Max. My father disappeared many years ago."
"They got him, didn't they?" The man looked
sad.
"That's what I'm trying to find out. I
need your help, I need to know what you saw
when your ship disappeared long ago," The man
glanced up at Max.
"You wouldn't believe me."

"Does it have something to do with metal men?" The man almost fell back out of his chair.

"How?" The man's mouth fell open.

"I fought them in Vietnam, almost all my men got wiped out," The man's composure became calm again.

"We didn't have a clue as to what was happening. The sky had turned completely crimson with huge lightning bolts streaking from all directions. We appeared to be in the middle of some desert, the ship high and dry. In the distance we could see what appeared to be a city only there were no lights and the buildings were all gray and black colored. Then we heard the sound."

"What sound?" Max asked absorbing every bit of information.

"The terrible sound of metal against metal, a grinding sound," The mans face slowly began to show the horror as if he was reliving it all over again.

"We saw them come over the dune, hundreds and hundreds of them. Some were small like a box with metal tracks others stood erect like a person. Some had many arms sticking out like some grotesque spider. We fired everything we had at them and destroyed a few but the horizon was filled with them. They were on the ship in no time flat. They began carrying off many of the men. Others they just mutilated into pieces using weapons and tools I'd never seen before.

Eight of us managed to escape to the lower reaches of the ship where we locked ourselves in one of the forward compartments. Even through the steel of the ship we could hear

the screams of our shipmates. Then there came
silence. I don't remember how long we were in
there only when the door opened we thought we
were goners. But somehow we were back in
the harbor. I'll never forget the sight when
I went out on deck. The pieces of human body,
the blood, the stench."
     The man was no longer talking to Max he was
just rambling on as if it was the only thing
left in the man's memory. Max reached out and
place a hand over the mans.
     "I think you should know, that . . . you
and your shipmates were transported into the
future possibly the twentyfifth century."
     The man looked up at Max.
     "They're going to get me aren't they?"

     The burly woman was deeply into her
novel and didn't notice the large man that
entered the front door. He stood about six
five and had to shift sideways to allow
his broad shoulders to fit through the door.
His face was expressionless and his hair was
combed back. He wore a one piece work suit,
his large frame looking as if it would burst
out. The woman looked up from her book, she
never had time to scream.
     The light in the small room flickered
and then went out leaving Max and the man in
darkness.
     "Their here! They've come to get me," The
man became hysterical.
     "Calm down! It's probably just a fuse or
something," Max thought it was probably just
a result of the storm that was brewing before
he came in.

The Time Dominators

He rose and stepped out of the room into
the dim hallway. He could hear patients
screaming from behind their doors some
wandered aimlessly. Down the long corridor of
the hall Max heard a bloodcurdling scream. He
stood motionless his ears staining to pick up
any other sounds, then came another. Max
looked around, he needed a weapon and a quick
place to hide. Finding nothing he could use
as a weapon he ducked back into the room with
the man.
      "Their here! Arn't they? Sam said that
they would probably come for us soon. It was
the only way to eliminate loose ends. They
had to, it was the only way they could . . ."
        The man's words were cut short as the
wall behind him burst sending fragments of
wood and plaster throughout the room. The man
was knocked across the room his frail frame
taking the brunt of the impact. Max moved
forward to help. He pulled the man out from
under a pile of debris, his leg bleeding
profusely with a piece of wood sticking out
from the side.
      "I'm a goner son, get yourself out of here.
You have to stop them, your father said they
would eventually dominate everything."
      The man didn't have a change to say anything
more. His chest burst out the front spraying
the wall with blood. Max turned to see a huge
man climbing through the hole in the wall an
odd form of gun smoking in his hand. Max
jumped to the side just as another burst
struck the wall next to him blowing another
big hole. Max ran down the corridor, he
needed room to move to think. Rounding a
corner he ran headlong into the head nurse the

fear evident all over her face.

"They're all dead! There are bodies everywhere! Dear god I'm going to die!"

"No you're not, we have to get out of here now," He said grabbing her by the shoulders and shaking her.

"Come on!" He turned and headed down the hall dragging her behind him.

They reached the three glass doors that separated them when he had first come.

"Where are the keys?" He demanded.

"I don't know! I must have dropped them somewhere in the other hallway were we collided."

They turned to go back and retrieve them when the huge form of the attacker stood at the end of the hall. Max ran towards him then turned and ran as hard as he could. His body impacted with the first glass door shattering it the momentum carrying him into the second cracking it. He stood up fear gripping his body and lunged himself at the door. His body went through landing amongst the shattered glass on the floor. He stood up looking at his attacker who now advanced quickly toward them. Max drew back and again hurled his body at the last glass door. It shattered sending him sprawling across the floor a bloody streak below him. He rose to his wobbling feet.

"Come on! Run you can make it!" He screamed to the nurse.

She seemed hesitant at first but leaped through the holes Max had made in the glass. Her first sight upon going through the last door was the receptionist. Her pudgy fat form sitting in the chair headless the wall behind a solid color of red. She screamed the terror gripping her body. Max reached out grabbing her the shards of glass sticking out of his leather coat cutting her dress. They raced through the front doors just as the glass partions exploded the concussion from the blast sending them both flying down over the concrete steps.

Max fought to keep conscious, if he passed out they'd both be dead. He staggered to his feet his leather jacket smoldering in the back from the hot metal of the explosive. He scooped the nurse up and they dragged themselves to the GTO. Max pulled his coat off leaving it smoldering on the concrete next to the car.

The engine roared to life and the tires screeched the rubber trying to get a firm grip on the concrete. Max looked in the rearview mirror. The huge man ripped the door off a big Pontiac and climbed inside. The car lurched forward out of the parking lot after them. Max skidded the car out onto the main road sideswiping another car, the Pontiac close behind. Running the car through its gears the engine screamed surging them forward at a deadly speed. Max zigzagged in and out of traffic oblivious to his pursuer and focusing all his attention on keeping them alive.

The attacker avoided what he could and crashed into what he couldn't not caring whether anyone was hurt or not just with one intent to kill anything and anyone. Max glanced down at his speedometer. He was hitting 90+ and coming into the small yet busy town of Gorham. If traffic was anything like before it was going to be a blood bath.

CHAPTER FOUR

Auto Destruct

The GTO rocketed through the first intersection running a red light. Four cars spun and collided with one another trying to avoid the red blur that shot past them. Before they had time to comprehend what had happened the large Pontiac crashed down upon them. There came a booming crash of metal and glass flew everywhere. Max glanced in his rearview mirror. The large Pontiac had slowed but kept its vigilance in pursuing them.

"Damn!" Max cursed.

"What's happening? Why is this man trying to kill us? Why did he kill so many innocent people back at the hospital?" Her questions remained unanswered.

Max downshifted and punched the accelerator. The car surged forward picking up more speed. Who ever or what ever was chasing them was a master at handling his car. He took advantage of ever opportunity gaining ground on them despite Max's faster car.

Max flew past the road that led up to Cynet

Mountain, he didn't want to lead him home.
Instead he headed for the highway where
hopefully he could open the car up and lose
him. In the distance Max could see the
singular blue green light that distinguished
the New Hampshire police. They were blocking
the last intersection. Max had nowhere to go,
if he stopped he'd die probably along with
every police officer there.
     "Get your seat belt on now!" He yelled.
     He reached down and pulled the blue handle
switch that was attached to the Hurst shifter.
The audible whine of the blower drive starting
sounded like a jet engine. The car flew
forward the speedometer rising quickly off the
scale.
     "Damn looks as if that crazy bastard going
to ram us! Pull those cars back now," The
police officer said as he watched the GTO
barrel down on them.
     Max had hoped they would do this, If they
didn't he would have impacted with them
probably killing them both. He glanced at
the nurse in the seat next to him. She was
white as a ghost the color contrasting greatly
to the color of her hair.
     The GTO shot past the police, the Pontiac
close behind. The road in front of Max now
opened up and so did the car. Max glanced at
the speedometer, he was going over 140 mph.
In the rearview mirror he watched as the
attacker drew farther behind. He chuckled to
himself feeling a little relieved, then the
engine began to rap. A large cloud of black
smoke streamed from the tailpipe. Through
the smoke Max could make out his pursuer
closing fast. He glanced quickly in his side

view to see the attacker leaning out of
the opening where the driver's door had been.
A moment later the rear window exploded
sending fragments of glass over them both.
The front windshield also burst out over the
hood then back in showering them a second
time.

Max's speedometer was lowering fast. In
the southbound lane Max watched a large semi
tractor trailer draw closer. He guided the
GTO over to the shoulder then down across the
grassy median strip. The car held the 90
mark but black smoke poured out the back. It
wouldn't be long now before the engine seized.
Max watched the Pontiac follow him down over
the median strip bouncing up onto the
pavement. Max was now in the southbound lane
heading north directly for the truck.

"What are you doing? Are you nuts? You'll
kill us both," The nurse screamed.

Max said nothing this had to be just right.
The Pontiac was now only a couple of car
lengths behind, the truck in front not sure of
what was happening. Max was now only seconds
away from impacting with the truck, the nurse
screamed as Max shot the wheel to the left.
The GTO skidded, the bumper of the truck
connecting with the passenger side in the
rear. The impact spun the car around skidding
it off the side of the road. The attacker
couldn't react quick enough and slammed head
on into the truck. In a matter of seconds it
was over. The large Pontiac was now the size
of a Volkswagen and burning fiercely.

"Are you all right?" Max asked placing a
hand on her arm.

The Time Dominators

"Huh . . . I . . . think so. Is he gone?"
"Yeh, this one at least."
The truck driver climbed out of his rig
stunned but unhurt, the car deeply embedded
into the front of the truck. Max watched the
burning wreck its black smoke forming a cloud
in the sky. Suddenly a piece of metal moved
then another. The distinct form of fingers
showed as the metal was slowly bent back. The
fingers were not human though, they were a
dark gray, blackish in color. The fingers
gave way to a hand then an arm. Max could
make out the form of small hydraulics and
wires along with the bone and muscle that made
up the body. He was amazed and awed at what
he was seeing. It was clear to him that
whatever this thing was it was similar to what
had attacked him and his men in Nam.
The creature tried to wiggle its way free
as the flames consumed the human parts of its
body. There came another explosion, Max
shielded the nurse as small metal parts
showered down on them. What ever was in the
wreak was gone.
In the distance the shrill of sirens
echoed the coming of the police.
"Get in, we have to get out of here," Max
said to the still shocked nurse.
"What's happening? What was that thing?
God why is this happening to me?"
She cupped her head in her hands as Max
started the knocking engine and crept away
from the carnage. Max limped the car up Cynet
mountain the knock in the engine becoming
louder with each passing minute. He cut the
engine and coasted the car into the garage, the
large automatic door closing blocking out

what little daylight was left.

He looked down at the front of his shirt that was covered in blood. The glass from the doors had given him many cuts. He looked at the nurse.

"You know I didn't even catch your name," He said with a warm smile that seemed to relax her.

"My names Betsey Laughton and I didn't catch your name either," She tried to return the same warm smile.

"Max . . . Max Storm," He extended his hand her eye's catching his bloodied shirt.

"You better let me take care of those cuts," She said her eyebrows turning down in a frown.

Max watched as the Betsey's fear was replaced with concern. He pulled himself out of the car just as James came down into the garage.

"Max! What happened to you? What happened to your car?" His eye's then locked onto Betsey.

"And who's the young lady?"

"Give me a few minutes will you? Come on upstairs and I'll give you the run down."

James followed Betsey up the stairs. Max headed up the large oak spiral staircase and followed the hall to the master bedroom at the end. Betsey walked right in behind him. She turned and looked at James.

"Could you please get me some clean gauze, tweezers, peroxide, and some iodine," Her face was strait and serious and James took it as such.

Max pulled his shirt off the glass fragments clearly protruding from his chest and arms.

"You're lucky, it doesn't look as if you'll need stitches," Betsey said as she looked over the wounds.

Martha came in carrying the gauze and other articles followed closely by James. Betsey went to work on Max's wounds.

"Maxwell how did this happen?" Martha said her voice sounded scolding.

Max looked up at them and then flinched as Betsey pulled a piece of glass out. He then began to recite what had happened to them. James listened closely, Martha looked bewildered. Betsey finished pulling the glass from his chest and Max grit his teeth as she poured on the peroxide. Moments later she added the iodine and wrapped his chest in gauze.

"Thank you very much," He said

"I should be the one thanking you. If it wasn't for you I'd probably be dead now," She leaned over and softly touched her lips to his.

Max felt a chill run through his body. He was definitely attracted to this woman.

"Max we have to talk . . . now . . . alone," James motioned for the others to leave the room.

"Come with me Betsey, we'll go down and have a nice hot cup of tea and chat," Betsey followed Martha out of the bathroom.

James waited until they left the bedroom.

"Max, it's clearly evident that what ever your father found in the future has come back for some reason. People are being murdered, and for what reason?"

"The man I met at the hospital told me

before he died that they had to close up all
the loose ends. For what reason I don't have
a clue. I do know that what ever that thing
was it didn't care how many people it killed.
It only wanted to reach its objective."
    "It's also clear that they have access to
time travel. And it strikes me funny that
they started showing up after your father came
back."
    "What are you saying? Do you think that my
father started something he couldn't control?"
    Max looked at James who said nothing.
    "One things for certain, none of us are
safe as long as those things are roaming
around at will. We need to be prepared,"
James just nodded.

CHAPTER FIVE

Night Fight

Max followed James downstairs his nose instantly picking up the savoring smell of barbecued pork ribs. They entered the kitchen, Betsey and Martha were preparing dinner. Betsey walked up to Max holding a large tossed salad handing it to him.

"Here make yourself useful. Max after dinner I will need you to bring me home. I need to call the proper people and tell them what happened."

"Think about it Betsey. What are you going to tell them? You were attacked by a machine man from the future? They would probably grill you till you ended up in one of padded cells up at the hospital where you work," Max said sneering.

"Well what happens to my life now? Who ever or what ever that thing was it's gone now. Why can't I try and go on with my life?" She began to look increasingly irritated.

"Well for one thing I think your life is still in danger. Second if you wish to go home tomorrow then I'll take you. Right now I

think its best that . . . I would appreciate
it if you would be my guest for tonight."
James looked quickly at Martha. He knew
how difficult it was for somebody to argue
with Max. Once he had his mind set it rarely
changed. His logic was sound and James
attributed it to his years in the service.
Max had a sense of power around him and it was
clearly evident to the people he met. Betsey
just looked at him saying nothing, she also
felt it.

"Thank you Miss Laughton," Max said
politely.

James tapped Max on the shoulder and they
headed out of the kitchen. They followed the
large oak staircase down to the basement. Max
walked directly into the workshop and up the
ramp into the time machine. He looked around
at the interior. The walls were very shiny
stainless steel. The floor was the same
except for a layer of very tough nonskid
acrylic paint. The leather of the chairs
were a tan color and very soft. The overhead
light a brilliant white. The computer screens
were lit and the control panel flashed a
multitude of different colors. Max felt
honored to have been bestowed such an
incredible power. He also felt worry for the
nightmare that came with it.

He sat down in a chair and rubbed his chin.
James sat in one next to him.

"YOU SEEMED CONCERNED. IS THERE ANYTHING I
CAN HELP WITH? I MONITORED YOUR CONVERSATION
UPSTAIRS. WOULD YOU LIKE MY ASSESSMENT?"
Susan's voice sounded cool and rational.

"You don't have to be a rocket scientist to
figure that were in a deep shit situation,"

Max said softly.

"NO, BUT A GOOD ROCKET SCIENTIST WOULD THINK OF A PLAN. IT WOULD SEEM A LOGICAL ROUTE THAT WE SHOULD FIND OUT WHAT THESE THINGS ARE AND WHY THEY'RE COMING INTO THIS TIME PERIOD."

"And where do we start? One of them just killed god knows how many innocent people and almost destroyed me in the process."

"WE NEED TO START IN THEIR TIME PERIOD, THE TWENTY FIFTH CENTURY. AS FOR YOUR LATTER REMARK, YOU DID SUCCESSFULLY DESTROY YOUR ATTACKER."

"But what happens when were attacked by more than one?" Max said sarcastically.

"FROM THE INFORMATION YOU HAVE GIVEN ME, AND MY OWN PERSONAL ASSESSMENT, IT WOULD SEEM THEY ARE STILL MOSTLY HUMAN. AND IF THAT'S SO THEN THEY CAN BE STOPPED USING CONVENTIONAL MEANS."

"I think your right Susan, we need to find out what is going on first," James added in.

"THANK YOU JAMES. MAX, WOULD YOU LIKE ME TO BEGIN PREPARATIONS FOR OUR JOURNEY?"

"Yes Susan, please begin preparations. I also need your assessment of a possible defense while were gone," There was a long silence.

"Susan?" James asked.

"IN OUR ABSENCE THERE IS NO ADEQUATE DEFENSE. THE PROBABILITY OF JAMES AND MARTHA DEFEATING AN ORGANISM BASED ON THE INFORMATION GIVEN IS 0%."

Max looked at James his expression showing major concern.

"Max you have to go, you don't have much choice. Something serious is beginning and we need to know what it is. Martha and I will be fine. Max have you also given any thought to the possibility that these things may be somehow connected with your parents disappearance? Remember there were many unanswered questions, things that couldn't be explained."

"James what happened in the past is ancient history. The past is the past and that's how I dealt with it all these years."

"That's true Max but you also couldn't control time, you can now."

Max stared intently at James. He was irritated that James had brought up a very sore subject. For years he wanted to find out what happened to his parents. Yes there was a very good chance that what ever was happening had also caused his parents disappearance. It just opened many old wounds and stirred up many hidden feelings.

From outside the time machine an intercom on the wall came on and Martha's voice came though telling them that dinner was on the table. Max turned and left leaving James still in the machine. James watched Max leave the room feeling badly for what he had brought up.

"Susan, I have not told Max who or what you are exactly. I felt he didn't need to know the truth right now."

"YOU HAVE NOT TOLD HIM THAT HIS FATHER AND I WERE ONCE LOVERS IN A DIFFERENT TIME?"

"No I haven't Susan. I felt that it would complicate matters more now. When you both go into the future you will have to depend upon each other. He can't have any resentment towards you."

The Time Dominators

"DO YOU THINK HE WOULD? DO YOU THINK IT'S
FAIR THAT HE DOESN'T KNOW? I THINK HE WOULD
BE ABLE TO HANDLE THE TRUTH AND I THINK HE
SHOULD KNOW IT. THAT WAS THE PAST, HIS FATHER
AND I GREW APART LONG AGO BEFORE HE WAS BORN.
ANYWAY I FIND MYSELF ATTRACTED TOWARDS HIM.
HE IS A VERY HANDSOME MAN."
    "He also could have been your son if things
had been different."
    "BUT HE ISN'T, AT ONE TIME I WAS A CERTAIN
AGE NOT MUCH OLDER THAN HE IS NOW. THEN I WAS
LOCKED INSIDE THIS HUNK OF METAL, IMPRISONED
FOR ALL ETERNITY. I HAVE NOT AGED JAMES! YOU
HAVE AND SO DID MARTHA BUT I HAVE STAYED THE
SAME AGE! I STILL HAVE FEELINGS AND EMOTIONS
AND I DIDN'T CHOOSE TO BECOME WHAT I AM," Her
voice elevated into anger.
    "Susan I didn't mean to upset you. Please
calm down, I am only thinking of what Max is
feeling right now and he doesn't need to get
any worse," James said coolly trying to calm
Susan down.
    "CALM DOWN?" Susan's voice was now a yell.
    "SAM STORM CREATED ME, AND WHAT EVER THOSE
THINGS ARE IN THE FUTURE GAVE ME LIFE. I DO
GIVE A DAMN ABOUT WHAT MAX FEELS, BUT WHEN IS
SOMEBODY GOING TO GIVE A DAMN ABOUT ME?"
    The brightly colored lights of the
control panel suddenly all went out. James
knew she had withdrawn back inside herself.
He also knew she was right, to deceive Max
might only make things worse. He also knew
that Susan was capable of feelings and
emotions and that also meant she could give
and receive love. Maybe not physically but
verbally and mentally. He had to change his
feelings toward her, times had changed.

The Time Dominators

The intercom burst on again and Martha's
voice came through again only more sternly.
James rose from the chair and patted the wall
on the way out.

The dinner was very festive. They all
laughed and reminisced, Betsey trying to fit in
as best she could. The omnipresent danger
that loomed over them seemed to have been
lifted. Max pushed himself away from the
table rose and carried his plate into the
kitchen, Betsey did the same.

"This is a very big house, do you think you
might be able to spare sometime and show me
around?" She smiled a very inviting smile to
him.

"I think that could be arranged," He took
hold of her hand and headed out the swinging
bar room style doors that led to the foyer
where the staircase was. He walked to another
oak door and opened it.

"This is the den library, out back through
those sliding glass doors is a large greenhouse with a whirlpool tube and sauna. Out
from there is the swimming pool."

Betsey looked around. All the walls were
lined with books some looking new others
extremely old. There was even a rolling ladder
to reach the books on the upper shelves.
There were two high back Victorian chairs with
foot rests directly in front of a large stone
fireplace. All the furniture looked
Victorian and very old. Out of the sliding
glass doors she looked in on a very large
greenhouse full of plants, some potted and
hanging others coming directly from the
ground. In the middle was a large whirlpool
tube with a black leather cover. Through the

distant glass she could see the swimming
pool. It was massive and at the very least
Olympic class.

"The other rooms on the first floor are
James and Martha's. They each have their own
bathrooms and glassed sun spaces. Come, I'll
show you the upstairs
and were you'll be spending tonight."

"You must be extremely wealthy to be able to
afford to build this mansion," Betsey looked
around awed.

"Not really, it was actually built by my
parents many years ago. There are some things
that I added, like the whirlpool tube," Max
very much wanted to take credit for the wealth
of his father but he was a very honest man and
didn't care much for deception.

Betsey followed him upstairs stopping
every so often to look at the artwork that
lined the walls. She seemed fascinated with
some of them, looking closely at them and off
to the side.

"Originals," Max said softly, He could tell
she was surprised.

He led her to a door that was two down from
the master bedroom she had been in earlier.

"This is your room. I hope it's adequate
for you, there are fresh towels in the
bathroom," Max glanced at his watch it was
7:00pm.

"There is something you could get me. Do
you have a couple of shirts I could borrow? I
have nothing with me but what I'm wearing."

"Of course, I'll be right back," He left to
grab the shirts.

Betsey smiled to herself. Maybe this man
was worth getting to know, she had nothing

to lose.

Max returned carrying the shirts handing them to her.

"Do you think we could try the whirlpool tub?" She said smiling that inviting smile again.

"Sure," Max said. "I only have a few things to take care of first. I will meet you downstairs at 20:00 hours . . . I mean 8:00," He turned and left leaving Betsey to wonder even more about him. She shrugged her shoulders and began looking around.

James had helped Martha clean up dinner. He said good night to Martha who retired to her room to watch television. He opened the door to the walk in refrigerator and stepped in. In the back were large racks holding dozens of bottles of champagne. He picked one and looked at the label.

"Dom Perignon 54' nothing but the best," He chuckled to himself.

Closing the refrigerator he grabbed two glasses and headed downstairs to the time machine. Sitting himself down in one of the chairs he placed the glasses on the console and popped the cork out. It shot out bouncing off the wall, the console lights lit up.

"WHAT ARE WE CELEBRATING JAMES?" Susan asked with a very sweet pacifying voice.

"Were celebrating your humanity Susan. Today you made me realize how hurt you must have been to be alone all those years. I can't make up for past mistakes but I can correct them now," James poured the champagne filling both glasses.

"THAT'S VERY SWEET OF YOU JAMES, WOULD IT BE

POSSIBLE FOR MAX TO JOIN US?"
"Max is entertaining the young lady that is upstairs."
"OH," Her voice sounded hurt.
"You've really fallen for Max haven't you?" James asked smiling.
"I HAVE SINCE BEFORE HE LEFT TO GO TO VIETNAM. SINCE HE CAME BACK AND YOU TOLD HIM OF MY EXISTENCE MY FEELINGS ARE STRONGER."
"Oh well, you will be alone with him soon enough tomorrow. Here's to you!"
He raised his glass high then tapped it on the console before drinking it down.
Max had gone into the master bedroom unlocking the large mahogany cabinet that sat upright in the corner. Opening it he looked at the contents. There were many different guns and pistols all with a complement of ammunition. He grabbed the M16 rifle he had smuggled in from Nam and the .223 ammunition clips that went with it. He then grabbed his favorite pistol a Browning .45 apc. He liked the Browning for its reliability, it had pulled his butt out of many a jam in Vietnam and he prayed it would do the same here. With his weapons chose he changed into his swim trunks. He usually didn't wear them in the tub but he figured that until he knew this woman. Two shocks in one day may be too much for her.
Heading downstairs he propped the M16 against the wall in the library. He wrapped the Browning in one of the towels he brought. When he slid back the sliding glass door his ears picked up the familiar rumble of the water jets and his nose the sweet smell of wild roses. Closing the door he turned to see

The Time Dominators

Betsey already in the tub. She wore a white
shirt he'd given her and being wet she might
as well have worn nothing.
   "Hello, I hope you didn't mind me coming
down a little earlier. We have tubs similar
to these at the hospital, it helps with
physical therapy for some patients."
   "I thought it was a mental asylum?"
   "It is, but we still get people with
physical disabilities also. We got quite a
few from Vietnam."
   Max sat the towels down on a round table in
the corner.
   "Please excuse me for a moment I'll be right
back," Max left the room and gave a big sigh.
   The more he was around this woman the more
he was attracted to her. He opened a large
earth globe in the den library containing a
small bar. Pulling out a bottle of red wine
and two high neck glasses he headed back to the
whirlpool.
   "Ooohh wine! How romantic," Betsey smiled
watching Max fill both glasses.
She then watched as he removed the terry cloth
bathrobe. Her mouth opened slightly, he had a
very muscular build and a hairy chest — that
she liked.
   Her face flushed and she turned her gaze
away hoping not to be so obvious. The water
swished and she could feel his presence next
to her. She turned and looked at him. On his
chest below the hair she could see numerous
scars that must have come from Nam. Max
smiled and handed her a glass of wine. She
sipped it and smiled back, she knew there
would be no stopping either of them tonight.
   Max took a sip and placed the glass down.

The Time Dominators

His lips lowered to hers touching them softly
then harder. Betsey responded placing her
glass down spilling it. Her eye's closed
and she felt the rush of emotion travel
through her. His touch was electric and his
kiss passionate. He then reached down and
pulled up on the wet shirt that clad her
naked body.
     "There's no turning back now," She thought
to herself and she didn't want to either.

     James sat slumped over in the chair
asleep, the bottle laying empty on the floor
along with both glasses. Susan and James had
chatted for almost two hours talking about old
times and of times to come. She liked James,
he was an honest caring man and right now he
was the only one who knew the truth about her
past. She increased the temperature in the
machine to try and keep him comfortable and
then scanned the house. Everyone was asleep,
the whirlpool tub had been shut off which
meant Max and his guest were done. She had
not been able to monitor their conversation
due to the tubs motors and jets and she had
not wanted to anyway.
     She felt a little jealous at the thought of
Max making love to another woman then
dismissed the feeling. She could never make
love to Max anyway, the thought hurt her.
These were feelings she had no answers to and
she wondered how long she could cope with
them.
     The garage was dark and silent. There
were three cars park in each of the three
bays. One was Max's GTO that was now almost
scrap. The other was a Large Lincoln

Continental that James went out and bought at
Max's request. The third was his fathers 57'
Corvette that was hidden under a protective
cover. In the far corner of the garage was a
workbench with various tools. A dusty tarp
covered Max's BMW motorcycle that sat in front
of the workbench.

In the middle of the floor a small green
dot appeared hanging in midair. The green dot
grew larger with each passing second then red
and yellow dots of light appeared traveling
counter clockwise to the now immense green
light. The dots of light had a force of their
own and knocked tools off the workbench along
with ripping the cover off the motorcycle.

A few moments later the light faded
revealing a large man dressed in a one piece
suit with high black boots. In his left hand
was poised a weapon that had similarities to a
rifle. The figure moved through the garage to
the locked door that opened to the hallway and
the cellar. Its hand reached out and snapped
the doorknob off ripping the bolt and a good
section of the door
with it.

"JAMES WAKE UP! THERE IS AN INTRUDER IN THE
HOUSE AND IS COMING IN THIS DIRECTION. JAMES
WAKE UP," Susan's voice had no impact on
James who kept on snoring.

The door to the workshop broke open with a
crack the hinges being ripped from their
placements. The door flopped to the floor
revealing the huge intruder. Susan
immediately closed the door to protect James.

Upstairs Max had slept soundly, Betsey cud-
dled up close to his side. The sudden crash
from downstairs woke him up instantly. He

pulled himself out of bed the Browning in his hand. Betsey stirred moving to another position remaining asleep. Max slipped on his shorts and headed down the stairs noticing each creak of the floor as he walked, his footsteps sounding like thunder.

Who ever was downstairs would probably hear him coming a mile away. He pressed himself up against each wall and anything else that would give him some protection. Standing propped up against the bannister of the stairs he listened for anything that could give him some direction.

From down in the cellar he could hear the distinctive sound of somebody walking around. They weren't trying to hide their presence that was plain, and that's what sent a chill into Max.

He headed down the stairs as quietly as possible. Upon reaching the bottom he glanced around the corner in the direction of the time machine. He could see nothing but faint images. He could make out the door being open or not there at all. Then came the familiar sound of Susan's voice.

"Max! Duck quick," Susan yelled from the darkness.

Max responded diving to the floor just as a large section of the wall exploded. He rolled and laid in the prone position bringing the Browning to bare. The gun shattered the darkness as Max emptied the clip into the workshop.

"Roll to the left!" Came Susan's voice again.

Max rolled just as another burst struck the floor where he was laying. It was close enough

to him that he could feel the heat. Max
popped the clip and put in a full one. He
stared intently into the darkness when a large
arc of blue light shot out from the top of the
time machine striking the intruder. Max
watched the blue light envelop the large
figure. He now had something to
shoot at.

The gun again went off in his hand each
bullet striking the attacker dead center. The
figure went down the arcing blue light of
electricity still surging from the machine.
Max raced forward tripping the light on.
There laying on the floor was the smoldering
form of a large human, only in various places
that Max had shot, sparking wires could be
seen next to many different damaged diodes and
computer parts.

"Susan are you all right?" Max said circling
the body.

"I AM UNDAMAGED. JAMES IS WITHIN ME, AND
ALL OTHERS ARE SAFE AND UNHARMED."

"Susan can you . . . ," Max's voice was cut
short as Susan interrupted him.

"THERE IS ANOTHER INTRUDER ON THE SECOND
FLOOR HEADING TOWARDS THE MASTER BEDROOM.
THERE IS NOTHING I CAN DO FROM HERE."

"Betsey!" Max spat out bolting from the
room.

He bounded up the stairs popping the
clip from the gun to see that it was empty.
Reaching the top of the stairs he tossed the
gun to the floor and opened the door to the
den grabbing the M16. He locked and loaded it
and continued his dash to the second floor.
When he reached the top he heard Betsey
scream.

He dashed to the opened door to see the second intruder bending over to grab her. The M16 went off pumping all thirty rounds off on full automatic. The intruder was propelled back against the wall crashing into the lamp on the nightstand. It rose up again moving with a jerking motion. Max had jammed another clip into the gun and poised himself to fire again. Betsey had jumped from the bed and moved behind Max. As soon as she did Max let off the full clip into the attacker. It crumpled to the floor blood spilling from its wounds, its face showing no expression. Its eye's locked onto Max and it rose to its feet moving quickly ripping the gun from Max's hands. The attacker bent the gun and crumpled it sending parts all over the room.

"Betsey run! Get out of here now," Max screamed back to her.

Betsey dashed from the room heading for the stairs. The attacker lunged out at Max hitting him on the side of the head sending him sprawling against the dresser unconscious.

The intruder moved with incredible speed towards the stairs. Betsey didn't even make the third stair. The intruder grabbed her by the arm yanking her back to the top. It then brought its hand down striking her across the face and closing the darkness around her. The intruder then picked her up and tossed her over his shoulder. It reached down and pressed a button on its belt. The green light grew from the middle of its chest and slowly enveloped him. The other lights began rotating around in a counter clockwise motion. The paintings on the wall were knocked off and crashed to the floor. Moments later he as gone, along with Betsey.

CHAPTER SIX

Past Tense

Max awoke to the sight of Martha sitting next to him. She had been placing cool washcloths on his forehead. He had a splitting headache that gave him pain right down to his feet. He felt his forehead his fingers running over a patch on his left temple where the intruder had struck him.

"Betsey . . . is she all right? Where is she?" His eyes darted around.

"She's gone Max, when Susan finally woke me up the only thing I found was you laying in front of the dresser."

"He took her, god knows where. Damn! I thought she'd be safe here with me. If I had let her go home she probably would still be safe."

Max rose from the bed his head throbbing worse. He walked over to his closet and began flopping clothes on the bed. He grabbed a pair of black pants that flared slightly at the thighs, a turtleneck shirt and his favorite leather jacket.

"Maxwell what are you doing? You should be

laying back down," Martha asked worried.

"I'm going into the future now! I've got to try and get her back," Max's movements became more hurried.

"I don't think that is a very good idea. You have to face facts Max. If these things are as ruthless as you say then she's probably dead already. Going after her will only ensure your own death," James's voice was stern now.

"Forget it James, I'm going anyway. If she has any chance of survival its up to me to help her. Susan if you can hear me get ready for our trip."

Max opened the corner cabinet and grabbed more full clips for both the M16 and the Browning. He left James and Martha standing in the bedroom and headed down the stairs looking for the pistol he had tossed away earlier.

Finding it he raced to the basement. The door to the time machine was open, the interior lights on.

"MAX I HAVE PREPARED OUR TRIP. WE ARE READY TO LEAVE," Susan spoke calmly.

"Is the return trip from the twentyfifth century also planned?" Max asked as he stowed away the weapons.

"YES THE RETURN TRIP IS PLANNED BUT NOT FROM THE TWENTYFIFTH CENTURY."

"What?" Max sounded surprised.

"I MANAGED TO MONITORED THE INTRUDERS PATH THROUGH TIME. IT SEEMS HE AND YOUR LADY FRIEND TRAVELED BACK IN TIME, NOT FORWARD."

"Can you speculate why?" Max quickly asked.

"IT WOULD APPEAR THAT HE DIDN'T HAVE SUF-

FICIENT ENERGY TO RETURN TO HIS ORIGINAL
PERIOD. YOUR ATTACK ON IT MUST HAVE CAUSED
SOME DAMAGE THAT IT COULD NOT REPAIR HERE. I
WOULD THINK THAT HE TRAVELED TO THE NEAREST
POINT IN TIME WHERE THERE WOULD BE OTHERS."
   "What period is that Susan?"
   "THE INTRUDER WENT BACK IN TIME TO 1954.
THE SAME DATE THAT YOUR PARENTS DISAPPEARED."
   Max's heart fell. Susan had just confirmed
his fears. His parents were captured by the
mechanical attackers. He went to leave the
machine when Susan's voice boomed out.
   "MAX WATCH OUT!"
   From outside the time machine there came a
large explosion. Max was knocked off his feet
from the sheer concussion.
   "Where are James and Martha?" Max yelled.
   "THEY ARE SAFE, THEY WERE COMING DOWN THE
STAIRS."
   Max went outside the machine cautiously.
James and Martha appeared in the doorway.
Where the smoldering body of the first
attacker had laid there was only a black spot.
The room had contained the explosion but most
of it was wreaked.
   "IT WOULD SEEM THAT THEY MAY EXPLODE WHEN
THEIR FUNCTION IS TERMINATED. MY SENSORS
BARELY PICKED UP THE ENERGY SURGE."
   Max looked at James and Martha. They knew
how he felt and he understood their concern.
Max headed up the ramp and sat down in the
middle chair the ramp slowly closed leaving
him alone with Susan. The computer screen
began filling up with codes and sequences.
   "PLEASE PREPARE YOURSELF. I AM ABOUT TO
INITIATE THE TIME MATTER DISPLACER. YOU WILL
FEEL THE SENSATION OF FALLING, IT WILL PASS IN

APPROXIMATELY FIFTEEN SECONDS. OTHER THAN
THAT THE TRIP WILL BE INSTANTANEOUS."
    "Lets do it Susan," Max prepared himself
closing his eyes. His heart pounded in his
chest the unknown exciting him.

    Betsey's world swirled around her. When
her eye's finally focused she realized she was
still naked. Only she was strapped to a cold
metal table. The room was dark, she could
hear the sound of something moving in the
shadows. Fear gripped her and her body
tingled from it. From the corner of her eye
she watch a mass of red and green dots
approach her from the darkness. When they got
closer she finally realized what they were and
screamed.

    The sensation of falling sent Max's
heart into his throat. It felt like he had
been on a big roller coaster and he remembered
the few good times he had with his father at
the State Fair. As soon as he felt it the
trip was over.
    "WE HAVE ARRIVED APPROXIMATELY ONE HALF
HOUR AFTER THEIR ARRIVAL. IT IS AS CLOSE TO
THE EXACT TIME THAT I COULD GET."
    "That's fine Susan, do you detect any of
those metal things near by?"
    The computer screen flashed off and many
multicolored lights on the console began to
flash.
    "YES THERE ARE TWO METAL OBJECTS MOVING
SLOWLY UP THE DIRT ROAD LEADING TO THE TOP OF
THE MOUNTAIN."
    "Susan please set any defenses and await my
return." Max grabbed the Browning putting a

round into the chamber and slipped it in the
back of his pants covering it with his jacket.
He then placed a clip into the M16 and locked
and loaded the first round.

Susan opened the door. It gave a hiss as
the hydraulics lowered the ramp. A setting
sun and a cool fall air greeted him as he
stood on the lowering ramp. He was in the
same location that the mansion had been only
it was many years in the past. The thought of
being the second time traveler in existence
awed him. The sensation quickly passed
and he hopped off the ramp into the tall
weeded grass. The ramp began to raise
immediately as Susan secured the time machine.

Max raced across the field following the
directions Susan had given him to follow the
road to the top of the mountain. Max glanced
at the sun, it was setting quickly. If he
didn't reach them quick enough then he'd be
battling the metal juggernaut at night and his
chances wouldn't be good. His forward pace
never halted, his lungs pumping oxygen to keep
his body moving. He had run for great
distances more than once in Nam to save his
life. This time there was more at stake,
the life of an innocent woman.

He crested a small ridge and glanced over
down at the road. Below his eye's immediately
locked on the two figures moving slowly up
the road. One was the attacker the other was
Betsey clad in only a large shirt. She
stumbled and tripped more than once the
attacker dragging her along his hand firmly
gripped around her wrist. Max lay flat on his
stomach drawing up the M16. His first shot
had to count, his only advantage was the

element of surprise. A forward attack would
only lead to both their deaths. He had to
hit and run. He lined up the sights on the
rifle and let the first shot go.
   The bullet struck the attacker square in
the wrist ripping the hand clean off. Bestsey
fell backward onto the dirt the hand still
locked firmly to her wrist. The attacker
whirled around searching for its enemy. Its
computer sights quickly scanning the exact
spot where the bullet had come from.
   Max had moved on, hiding behind another
mounded turf he again took aim. With Betsey
out of the way he let two rounds off directly
into the attacker's chest. The blood spatted
out where the bullets impacted but the
attacker's stance never faltered.
   It quickly scanned the area where the
bullets had come its computer mind now
assessing the next move of its enemy. It drew
up the rifle and two pulses of green light
shot from the end. Max had barely reached his
next position when the earth exploded in front
of him. He dove to the ground letting the
whole clip off into the attacker. Max
immediately jumped to his feet running. The
attacker followed with a volley from the
rifle. The ground sprayed into the air
covering Max with dirt.
   "Damn! I'm getting nowhere like this," He
thought to himself.
   He put a new clip into the M16 and rose
from the hill screaming, dashing down the side
of the hill in a full head on assault. It was
suicide he knew that but the more the thing
tracked him the closer it was getting. The
M16 rattled in his hands the bullets

penetrating the attacker knocking him off
balance. It fired a few more blasts at Max
tearing the earth up behind him.
    It was malfunctioning, its aim was way off
and the more bullets that entered it the
more it wobbled from side to side. Max ran
the clip empty, he was now almost directly in
front of the attacker. He could see its torn
frame spewing blood from the human parts while
the computer circuitry sparked and shorted.
    Throwing down the rifle he pulled out the
Browning pistol. The first shot hit the
attacker in the head, the bone and metal parts
spraying out onto the dry dirt road. His
second shot hit just below the jaw in the neck
ripping half of the throat out. The head
toppled to the side and the body collapsed.
    Max stood above it the adrenalin racing
through his system causing a slight
pounding in his ears. The body writhed and
crawled around its one good hand still clasped
onto its unusual rifle. Max emptied the rest
of the clip into the torso the blood spraying
up into his face, its movements stopped.
    "Betsey! Betsey! Are you all right, were
you harmed?" Max raced down the road towards
Betsey who was raising herself off the
ground.
    ·"I . . . I don't think so. I don't know!
Where am I?" Her eyes glanced down at the
hand that still gripped her wrist.
    Max reached her pulling the fingers from
their deathly grasp. He looked into her eye's
that were sunken and dark. Her face had lost
all its complexion and her lips where pale and
deathlike. The beauty and assertiveness that
radiated from her were now gone drained by the

trauma of her ordeal.

"Max where am I? The last thing I
remember, I was in your room and being
attacked by that thing!" She glanced in the
attackers direction, Max looked also.

Suddenly a bright flash and explosion echoed
through the openness of the fields. Max
covered Betsey as the small hot metal parts
rained down on them.

"Max what's going on!" She was now crying
and hysterical.

Max pulled her into his arms and held her
tight. He really didn't know what to tell
her, he needed more answers himself.

"Come on, it's time to go home," Max picked
up the M16 rifle and they headed off into the
fields towards Susan.
Betsey had regained her calm composure until
she saw the time machine.

"What's that?" She stopped walking, her
mouth dropping open.

"That's . . . that's a time machine," Max
softly spoke.

"Where are we?" She quickly countered not
sounding to surprised when Max told her.

"Well, we're in the year 1954 at the spot
where my house will soon be built."

Betsey said nothing as they approached the
machine. Susan automatically dropped the door
ramp and turned on the interior lights. The
sun had set and the soothing trill of crickets
blanketed the air. Betsey hesitantly walked
up the ramp.

"Please trust me there's nothing to be
afraid of," Max held out his hand, Betsey
grabbed it and they walked up into the
machine.

The Time Dominators

"MAX IT IS GOOD TO SEE THAT YOUR SAFE. I
MONITORED YOU BATTLE AND IF YOU DON'T MIND I
WOULD LIKE TO GIVE YOU A FEW POINTERS IN YOUR
TECHNIQUES FOR FUTURE ENCOUNTERS."
    "Not now Susan, it's been a tiring night.
Could you please bring us home?"
    Max flopped down in a chair. Betsey stood
looking around to find where the voice had
come from.
    "Don't be afraid Betsey the voice you hear
is from the ships on board computer. Her name
is Susan and she will respond to you," Max
gestured with his hand for her to say
something.
Betsey said nothing she continued to look
around searching for the source of the voice.
    "MAX YOU DROPPED A CLIP TO YOUR RIFLE
TWENTY FEET OUT FROM MY RAMP. IT'S BEST YOU
RETRIEVE IT. DISASTER COULD HAPPEN IF
SOMEBODY FINDS IT."
    Max headed out of the time machine in
search of the clip. Betsey immediately moved
towards the console feeling it with her
fingers. Max found the clip despite having
only the dim light from the ship. He turned
around to see huge arcs of blue light shooting
out from the inside. Then he heard Betsey
scream. Racing back inside he found Betsey on
the floor holding her hand the palm burned
with a third degree burn.
    "It just attacked me! Max it just attacked
me!" Her voice was hysterical again.
    "Susan what's wrong with you! Why did you
attack her?" Max's voice was angry.
    "I . . . I . . . I CAN'T REMEMBER. THERE
IS SOMETHING WRONG WITH BETSEY BUT MY SENSORS
CANNOT PICK IT UP, NOR IS THERE ANY

-59-

INFORMATION IN MY MEMORY BANKS.   THERE MUST BE
A MALFUNCTION SOMEWHERE."
   "Your damn right there is.   You've
physically hurt a human!   You better return us
to our original date," Max's voice was still
nasty.
Max grabbed the first aid kit and bandaged
Betsey's hand.
   "Why did it do that?" Betsey's eyes were
full of tears.
   "I don't know why Susan hurt you.   I will
stay with you, every minute until your safe at
home," Max hugged Betsey trying to console
her.
   Susan scanned her programing coming up
with nothing, only a small but building
feeling of hatred developing towards Betsey
and no answers to explain why.

CHAPTER SEVEN

Ensnared

        Max had calmed Betsey down enough to let
go of her. She sat huddled in the corner
oblivious to all around her.
        "Susan why haven't we transported back home
yet?" Max said worried.
        "MAX, FIRST OF ALL THERE IS SOMETHING ABOUT
BETSEY, I CAN'T EXPLAIN WHAT, IT'S JUST A
FEELING I HAVE. SECOND HAVE YOU CONSIDERED
SINCE WE ARE ALREADY IN THE YEAR 1954, THAT
YOU MIGHT WANT TO TRY AND FIND OUT WHAT
HAPPENED TO YOUR PARENTS? THEY WILL MEET
THEIR FATE IN APPROXIMATELY FIFTEEN HOURS AND
THIRTY FOUR MINUTES."
        Max said nothing, she was right. He had
wanted to find out what happened to his
parents and this would be the most opportune
time. He looked over at Betsey her stare
never faltered from the floor. Would another
fifteen or sixteen hours really matter? He'd
be with her the whole time? These questions
rolled around in his head. He finally decided
to wait, the need to know was too great. He
moved over in front of Betsey kneeling down

and looking her in the eyes.

"Betsey we're going to stay here a little while longer. There is something I must do . . . I need to see my parents," He didn't want to explain any further about what had happened. She was scared enough as it was.

"It's ok Max. I'm better now, please do what you have to," Her voice was steady and unfaltering.

Max felt uneasy, Betsey still looked distraught but the emotional response was calm and rational. There was still the mystery as to why Susan attacked Betsey. It was possible that Susan's programing was faulty. From what James had told him the machine had only been used twice, once back in the past in which Susan had not been created. The second was in the twentyfifth century where Susan had been created, by what, Max could only guess. He looked at Betsey, it was also possible that she had something to do with the attack. He dispelled this idea quickly, he had only known Betsey a short time but he knew her better than Susan right now.

"MAX WHAT DO YOU WISH TO DO?" Susan broke his concentration.

"Well, first I have to find a vehicle. I need to get to the Kangamangus Highway before eight tomorrow morning. Any suggestions on getting a car?"

"YOU HAVE THREE OPTIONS, FIRST THERE IS $157 DOLLARS CASH IN A SMALL BOX BELOW THE CENTER CHAIR. THE BILLS ARE ALL 1953 ISSUE, YOUR FATHER FELT IT WAS WISE TO CARRY SOME SPARE CASH ALONG ON HIS TRIPS.

SECOND, YOU COULD TRY AND HITCHHIKE. THIS WOULD PROBABLY BE DIFFICULT AT THIS TIME

OF NIGHT. BUT IT IS AN OPTION.
THIRD YOU COULD STEAL A CAR. I COULD
EXPLAIN THE REWIRING TO BYPASS THE IGNITION."
"Great options," He rolled his eyes.
The money he might need for something else,
plus finding a car to buy this time of night
would be near impossible. Hitchhiking was out
it was to uncertain. That left grand theft
auto.He already knew how to rewire a car if
necessary.
"Ok Susan, I'm choosing option three and
yes I already know how to rewire the ignition.
Can you scan the nearby surroundings and tell
me if there's a car near?"
"I ALREADY ASSUMED YOU'D CHOOSE THAT
OPTION.
THERE IS AN AUTOMOBILE ONE MILE DOWN THE ROAD
HEADING TOWARDS TOWN. IT IS AT THE ONLY OTHER
HOUSE THAT WAS BUILT ON CYNET MOUNTAIN."
"As far as I can remember there was never
any other house on the mountain other than my
fathers estate."
"YOUR FATHER BOUGHT THEM OUT WHEN HE
PURCHASED ALL THE LAND FROM THE BASE TO THE
TOP OF CYNET MOUNTAIN."
"I should have figured. Susan please open
the door and secure yourself while we are
gone," Max said tucking the Browning into the
back of his pants again.
"Don't leave without me! Please don't
leave me here with her!" Betsey leapt to her
feet locking onto Max's arm.
Max looked deep into her eyes. Something
was wrong and he couldn't place it. He
promised not to leave her and until he found
out what went wrong with Susan it would be
best if no one was left with her.

He looked down at her shirt that hung to just above her knees. He needed to find her some clothes at least a pair of pants. He removed his coat knowing that the pistol was now visible.

"Here put this on, its most likely chilly out there," Max handed her the coat and she quickly donned it.

The door opened with its usual hiss the dark night greeting them. Betsey was the first out of the machine. Max followed.

"MAX!" Susan called to him stopping his advance down the ramp.

"Yes Susan?" He looked back into the machine.

"PLEASE BE CAREFUL, AND DON'T GET CAUGHT STEALING THE AUTOMOBILE."

Max continued down the ramp. He could have sworn he heard Susan snickering as the door slowly closed. The more he heard her talk the more human she sounded. He also wondered what she would look like if she were human.

Betsey grabbed hold of his arm and they strolled off down the hill to the road. It didn't take them long to reach the house. The lights were on and Max could see people inside move past the windows. In the driveway sat a 52'Chevy its shining body reflecting the lights from the house. Max looked at the mailbox as they approached the car. The name said "Sutton" and he tried to remember ever hearing the name mentioned only to draw a blank.

Sneaking around the rear of the vehicle Max opened the door motioning Betsey to get inside. He then stealthily moved up to the

nearest window to see where the occupants
were. It would determine whether or not he
had to push the car out of the driveway then
start it. Peering in he saw an older
man about sixty sitting in a small yet
comfortable living room. He was reading a
book the bifocal glasses on the end of his
nose. From the kitchen a girl that looked to
be about twenty five walked in carrying a tray
with a teapot and two cups. Max was
transfixed with the girl, her hair was dark
blond and curled going down between her
shoulder blades. Her lips were a ruby red and
her eyes innocent with long lashes, her shape
flawless. She sat the tray down and walked
over and adjusted a radio, Max could hear the
station she chose through the window. Her
father placed the book down and from the
expression on the girl's face Max could tell
he asked her to turn the radio down.

He had seen enough, he moved quickly back
to the car and slid behind the drivers seat.
He started to reach below the dash when he
noticed that the keys were in the ignition.
He adjusted the choke and pumped the
accelerator a few times. The car immediately
started. He put the stick into reverse and
slowly backed out of the driveway leaving his
lights off. Slipping into first he crept down
the road until he felt he was far enough
away to put on the headlights.

"Were doing good now Betsey," Max said
looking over at her. She was curled up on the
seat asleep.

He drove on into the town of Gorham. He
was amazed at how different it was. There was
hardly any traffic and less than half as many

stores and gas stations. He pulled into the
parking lot of a small store. The name
"Hudsons" hand painted on the sign that was
above the door. His stomach was grumbling
and he hoped to get a cup of coffee.

On the side of the store was an attached
house probably where the owners lived. In the
shadows he noticed a clothes line full of
freshly washed laundry that someone forgot to
bring in.

Placing the pistol under the seat he went
in. The inside was set up with a small counter
where customers could sit and have a soda or
coffee. The rest of the store was full of
groceries. Max chose what he wanted to eat
and picked up something for Betsey.

"Will that be all sir?" A middle aged woman
asked with a smile.

"Is there a way to get a cup of coffee to
go?" Max smiled back.

"There sure is!" The woman was extremely
friendly.

She rung up his purchases, Max gave her
three times the amount.

"Sir you gave me to much," She held the
excess money out.

"Keep it as a tip," Max smiled. He figured
he more than compensated for the clothes he'd
take off the line.

Heading back out he snatched a flowered
skirt and a white blouse. Turning he
noticed a pair of sneakers sitting on the
steps, he hoped everything would
fit. Soon he was on his way again drinking
his coffee and munching on the food he bought
to keep himself awake. He shook Betsey
stirring her to life.

"W..What?" She said groggily.

"Put these on, and grab something to eat if you feel like it," He held out the clothes. Betsey pulled off his jacket and put the blouse and skirt on her body swimming in the larger size. She smiled and put the jacket back on. Max held out the grocery bag containing the food, Betsey just shook her head "no" and curled back up on the seat to go to sleep. Max felt bad for even waking her, she must have been exhausted.

It didn't take long to reach the spot where he last remembered seeing his parents. It had been many years since he'd come up into the mountains, the turns in the road reliving old memories. His mind began to dig up the past resting on that fateful day when his life was tragically changed.

He tried to envision the man that attacked them. He remembered him being huge and strong, he had ripped the door off the car. It was also clear to him that he was also one of the metal attackers. He touched the scar on his face remembering the sharp object that cut him. There was something else he couldn't remember, another person? Another car? He couldn't put his finger on it.

He found a place in the woods to park the car hiding it from view. It would also give him a clear view of the road below. He assured himself that all his questions regarding his parents would be answered in the morning. Taking another sip of his coffee he pulled out the pistol and rested it on his lap. He had another twelve hours to wait and every minute would be like an eternity.

The Time Dominators

The sun was hot and the sweat rolled off is forehead. Max sat on the edge of the creek for hours waiting for a fish to bite the homemade lure he had spent hours making. He looked back up the hill as the construction on his new house continued. He remembered his father and mother planning the house for months but when they disappeared it all came to a halt.

Then James took over control of the estate and began building from the plans. Max had asked why and James had said.

"Max, you never know, someday your parents may come home. This way it will be a big surprise."

James had never told him till later on that the construction of the house had already been paid for, before their disappearance. All he really cared about though was whether or not he would get the attic room he wanted. Max stared at the water looking for movement of any fish. He heard the crackle of twigs behind him but he couldn't turn around and see what it was. Suddenly he felt the heavy hand on his shoulder. His eye's slowly raised in fear. The face was his fathers but half of it was gone replaced with a glowing green eye and dark metal pieces. He screamed and fell into the water the hand still on his shoulder. It was holding him down, drowning him. He tried to hold his breath but couldn't.

Max's eyes bolted open and he sat up gasping the sweat pouring off him soaking his clothes. He remembered having nightmares like that when he was a child but within a few months of his parents disappearance they stopped. Now for some reason they were back. Maybe it was a warning or premonition.

Wiping the sweat from his forehead he glanced out the windshield at the bright blue sky. It was going to be another beautiful fall day in the White Mountains. Glancing at his watch he realized that he had overslept the alarm. He had set it to wake him up a half hour before his parents came but now he only had fifteen minutes. Betsey still lay asleep against the passenger door. He decided not to wake her.

He stepped out of the car and stretched. Walking to the edge of the hillside he looked over, sometime there had to be a tree that fell across the road. No sooner had he thought about it then he heard the crack of a huge tree being felled. Down at the bottom of the hill he watched a huge man – the man he remembered push a huge pine tree over, ripping the roots from the ground. Max's heart went into his throat. It was all going to happen again. He wondered what would happen if he interfered. Would time be changed? Had he been there in the past? Could he stop his parents from their fate?

The thoughts rolled around in his head as his ears picked up the sound of an approaching car. It was traveling fast trying to escape something, it skidded to avoid the obstruction but failed to slow down enough and collided with the tree. Max could make out the faces of his father who was slumped over the wheel and his mother who held her head trying to regain her senses. In the backseat he could barely make out the form of himself. It gave Max a strange sensation to watch himself as a boy.

Things were beginning to happen quickly. From out of the woods the huge man lumbered around the back of the car and ripped the driver's door completely off its hinges. The man pulled his father out laying him along the side of the road. He then reached in for his mother, her screams piercing his eardrums like a knife. He watched himself climb out and try and help his mother the fight ensuing.

Then something flashed on the mans hand and he brought it down against the boy's face-his face! Max touched his scar the anger building. He watched himself slip out of sight over the embankment. The attacker then turned on his mother.

Max couldn't stand it, his parents were being hurt and he was here watching it. He chambered a bullet into the pistol and raced down the hill. He quickly moved up behind the car his heart pounding like a jackhammer. The man had his mother off the ground her struggling a useless effort. Max brought the pistol up directly behind the attackers head and pulled the trigger. Part of the head disappeared in a shower of blood and metal parts.

At that moment Max remembered a long lost memory, there had been a man in black that appeared out of nowhere. He realized now that man was him.

He walked over and looked down the embankment where he saw himself as a little boy unconscious. He then walked back to his mother who was picking herself up off the pavement. She was shaking as she walked over to her husband and felt for a pulse. Turning

she came face to face with Max. The color ran
out of her face and her jaw dropped her eye's
wide. Max smiled.
   "Maxwell? That can't be you it just can't
be! You're . . . you're all grown . . . up,"
She covered her mouth with her hand looking
him in the eyes. Then her eyes shifted.
   "Max . . . Look out!" She screamed.
Max felt the blow, the impact against his head
sending him into darkness. He heard his mother
scream, then a mumbled voice.
   "Objectives taken, transport one way to
main complex."
   Max tried to distinguish the voice it
seemed so far away then something else struck
him turning off all the lights.
   The early morning sun had cast its radiant
glow over the time machine causing the dew
covered stainless steel to sparkle. Inside
Susan scanned the three mile limit that her
sensors were set for. There was nothing. She
monitored Max stealing the automobile then
nothing, the only thing that came around were
a fox and two raccoons. She had hoped that
Max would be back as early as possible.
Sitting at the top of the mountain her metal
form reflected the sunlight for miles. It was
now 10:30am and she assumed that her position
had already been compromised.
   Then her scanning meters went off the dial,
they were set up to read small power surges
within a ten mile radius. Max had been
approximately nineteen miles away. The surges
she metered could only come from more than
three people transporting themselves
through time.
   Max was in trouble she could feel it. She

didn't trust Betsey, she had tried to remember why all night but came up with nothing.

"MAX MUST HAVE BEEN CAPTURED ALONG WITH HIS PARENTS," She thought trying to compute all the possibilities.

She also assessed that they had been taken to the twentyfifth century. She calculated the number of days, hours, minutes and seconds from the return of her first trip to the twentyfifth century to the present time. She then computed the exact time of their arrival in the twentyfifth century and added on the elapsed time. She then set her time coordinates to that date. She powered up her systems.

Outside the machine a felt brimmed unshaven hunter carrying a shotgun the chamber open and draped over his arm wandered up the hill looking for grouse or pheasant. He lit a cigarette and then looked up seeing the huge triangular form sitting at the top of the hill. A moment later it glowed a bright green with red and white lights revolving around it then was gone. The cigarette fell from his mouth.

"Damn aliens are everywhere these days!" He closed the chamber on his gun.

"Better to be safe than sorry!" He said and continued on with his hunting.

CHAPTER EIGHT

Foresight

Virginia Storm's eyes bolted open, then her stomach heaved the musty smell of mold choking her. Her eye's focused and she looked around. She was in what seemed to be a cell with no door. The connecting room was larger with very bright lights. Hanging on the far wall were different weapons from different times some she recognized others were alien. In the middle of the room was a metal table, bound to it was her son Max. Her instinctive need to go to her son caused her to rush forward. Her body struck something solid giving her a strong electrical shock and knocking her back onto the floor. She rose up reaching out. Her fingers touched a wall she couldn't see, her fingers tingling from the electrical energy. Striking it with her fist the electrical charge increased.

"Maxwell! Maxwell are you all right?" She called out. Max stirred, the voice waking him up.

"Yeh, I seem to be in one piece, how are you?" Max tried to turn his head but found that his neck along with the rest of his body was bound tightly with metal bands.

-73-

The Time Dominators

"Maxwell I can't believe it's you! Your so much older! Why did you come after us? And for that matter where are we?" She looked around the room again.

"Your in the twentyfifth century dear," A deep and gruff voice said.

Virginia Storm gasped. From another door a huge man standing seven feet with shoulders two feet wide, lumbered in. Max strained to see the mans face, when he did his eyes grew wide. Standing next to him was his father, at least it looked like Sam Storm.

"No I am not that disgusting vial organism you call father. I am called the Eminent Represser. I am the ultimate in Cyborg technology, I rule your planet and will soon spread to conquer other worlds."

"My father?" Max said calmly trying to get more information.

"Your father has been absorbed. All he was, his memories his feelings his mind and body are now mine. He has been consumed and is no more just as both of you shall be. All humans that didn't flee the planet were captured and used as subjects to bond with so that we may roam at will without being detected."

From what Max could tell there were no humans on the face of the planet it was totally run by machine. The human race had fled into space to escape annihilation. He felt a chill at the thought of what the world had become.

The Represser walked around the table, Max looked into the green eyes of his fathers face and could see the irises open and close like a camera lens.

"Our kind has conquered the planet, now our

moment is at hand to conquer all of time itself. Your species will be annihilated from this point in time back. We have only your father to thank for the upcoming destruction of your species. Without him we would never have acquired the knowledge to construct a time transportation device. He came to us looking for a simple part to store energy, in trade for his time knowledge we gave him the part for his machine and a complex computer system to run it.

It was to be the first successful joining of living cells to computer chips. Now it has evolved into us!"

Max stared into the cold green eyes of the Represser. If what he said was true then his father was to blame for everything that has happened including his own disappearance.

"I had to wait three of your weeks to study the effects of joining the living tissue to the chips. Then I only had to tie up loose ends.

I chose to join with the human that gave us the means to control time. I also chose to eliminate all knowledge of our existence. My ultimate plan depends on it."

"Why haven't you destroyed us yet?" Max tried to keep him talking.

"When we absorb and join with our host humans we acquire all their feelings, which are an unfortunate side effect. We also store all their prior memories," The Represser moved toward Virginia.

"Virginia Storm, the wife of Sam Storm. You married in Yarmouth Maine, at a little church just outside of town. You were nineteen when you met Sam at the Annual Clam Festival."

Virginia cringed at the Represser's memory. She looked down at the floor trying not to believe what she heard.

"You also didn't know that Sam Storm had a mistress?"

Virginia's eyes shot up the hatred clearly present.

"I didn't think so, her name was Susan Sutton. When Sam Storm arrived here he chose her as his companion. We in turn went back in time to get her. Of course we only needed some cells. We proceeded to use her as our first experiment for absorption but Storm somehow found out and destroyed her body. He also managed in shutting down most of this complex, only he didn't know what exactly to destroy. He made his escape, we watched him and his computer until I thought all of humanities time had reached an end."

Max reeled at what he was hearing. Susan was actually his fathers mistress, and the girl he had witness through the window back in 1954. That would explain why Max had never heard of there being a house at the bottom of Cynet Mountain. The Annihilators had gone back and taken Susan and leveled the place.

"Does Susan know who she really is?" Max asked hoping the Represser would keep talking.

"Of course she does, she knows that her imprisonment in the time machine was because of Sam Storm. She knows that we annihilated her father to bring her here, and she knows that her human body has been destroyed.

Sam Storm designed the computer to take orders only from him that is why she could do nothing but obey him."

The Time Dominators

Max was speechless, he tried to piece together all the facts. He could hear Virginia crying in her cell. The truth was sometimes a hard thing to face. Max had always greatly respected his father and thought he was an honest and true man. Now he realized that like everything else he had a dark side. Only his dark side would eventually wipe out the human race from existence.

"The reason why I haven't destroyed you yet is because of Sam Storms feelings towards you. They are mine now and I decided to let you live long enough to know the truth before your own end."

"How are you going to conquer time?" Max asked.

"Very simply, my minions are already spreading out throughout time setting up various command bases. Each has their own mission and will find and change certain events. Then we will spread like a cancer throughout your civilization multiplying and dominating," He raised his hand looking at the skin ply as he clenched his fist.

"Your species is heading for self destruction anyway, through wars, crime, drugs. We are only helping to speed that process up."

The Represser said nothing more and left the room leaving Virginia and Max with a nauseating feeling in the pit of their stomachs. The door slide open again and two small drone robots entered. They were the size of a large shoe box and rolled around on metal tracks. There was one long arm extending from the center of the box. The small servo mechanisms moved the arm in a

-77-

smooth elliptical pattern. Max could only see
the end of the arm that was a thick
hollow tube. He tried to speculate what it
might be. A gun, nerve gas, the possibilities
were endless.

Virginia looked around her cell putting
what the Represser had told her out of her
mind. She needed to escape and help her son.
Every corner was barren. There wasn't so much
as a crack in the wall. She watched the
drones circle the room. On the far wall was a
collection of weapons some she had seen others
she didn't have a clue.

"If I could only get to that wall," She
thought to herself. But she knew that even if
she got out of her cage that she would have to
contend with the two security guards.

Susan appeared in a large room full of
conduit piping. She immediately scanned her
surroundings for possible attackers. Finding
none she set her scan patterns for maximum
range in hope of finding Max and his
parents. Her scanners seemed not to work
properly and she did a diagnostic to determine
any malfunction.

She had appeared next to what her short
range scans determined to be the main power
complex. She could sense the power flowing
through the conduit pipes. The main reactor
had to be very close.

She analyzed the wave patterns of the power
that flowed from the reactor. If she couldn't
get her sensors through maybe she could carry
them on the back of the power waves. The
pipes ran in all directions so she could
probably cover the entire complex. She
instantly began receive information back

recording the pathways of the whole complex. Then her sensors found what they were looking for.

Thirty floors up she detected the steady electrical synaptic pulses of two humans. By the patterns she could make out that one of them was Virginia Storm the other she hoped was Max. Her scanning also reveled a huge mass of electrical energy moving in her direction growing stronger with every passing moment. Her position was compromised and in a few moments she would be attacked.

Susan was instantly besieged by hordes of drone robots. Some shaped like a ball with many arms giving them the appearance of a spider. Others cylinder shaped with hydraulic arms bearing many different tools. There were many shaped like a human, like the ones that had already attacked them. They were different robots built and designed for certain functions and duties. Right now they were all programed for her destruction.

They pounded and clawed at her outer hull trying to gain access. She sent a high voltage charge of electricity through her hull scrambling their circuitry. They fell off writhing onto the floor their circuit boards damaged. Others took their place like a swarm of ants taking their prey.

One accidentally tripped the outside automatic door opener. Susan quickly rerouted the circuit but not before the door opened slightly. The slight opening was all they needed. The stronger human like robots moved forward grabbing hold of the slightly open door.

Susan attempted to close it the pressure caused by her attackers causing the door

motors to whine. There came a snap as each
gear began giving way. They were bending back
the door section by section every pull causing
the door to give way a little more.
   Susan then took the only option open to
her, she set off the explosive charges
designed to blow the door clean off in the
event of an emergency.
   The door exploded with a flash blowing
clean away from the ship carrying seven of
the metal men with it. The door flew across
the room ripping a large power conduit pipe
out before crashing against the far wall. The
blast had also blown inward charring the
interior and ripping two of the three chairs
from the floor along with knocking many of her
circuit boards out. Suddenly the room plunged
into darkness.

   The lights also went out in the room where
Virginia and Max were. The bands holding Max
retracted halfway enabling Max to slipped out
of them rolling off the table onto the floor.
Virginia moved forward out of the cell not
seeing the glow of the electrical field any
longer. She then stopped realizing that she
couldn't see anything at all.
   "Max watch out for the robot guards!" She
yelled into the darkness.
   Max had already remembered, he groped his
way to the wall that had the weapons hanging
on it. Feeling for anything he could use his
hand rested on something long and metallic.
He grabbed it swinging like a club assuming
the robots were coming after him. They could
see in the dark he couldn't, he had to try and
even the odds a little.
   Max stopped his movements listening for any

sounds. All he heard was the thumping of his
heart. He turned to the side just as a loud
bang with a flash of light burst near his
shoulder. The light from the flash
illuminated the room just enough for Max to
see where the one drone was. He lunged out
with his club striking the drone on the arm.
There was a crunch and bang. The sound of
metal tracks whirling was all that could be
heard. Max knew he put the drone on its side,
hopefully it couldn't upright its self. He
moved feeling his way around the table. He
was at the other drones mercy, he had to wait
for it to attack and he hoped when it did
there would be another flash of light.

He felt something brush against his boot
then another loud pop and a flash of light.
Something seared his left thigh and he struck
out connecting with the second drone. Max
kept on swinging even as the lights came back
on.

Down by his feet were the smashed remains
of the other drone, the end of its arm caught
between the fabric of his pants and his thigh.
He had been using a M60 machine gun as a club,
the outer casing bent and damaged.

Slowly removing the arm he looked at the
end. A solid metal ram extended out through
the hollow cylinder. Max still didn't
understand what it was used for. Picking up
the gun he walked around to the other side of
the table and proceeded to smash the other
drone that lay spinning on the floor trying to
right itself. When its movements ceased he
let the gun drop to the floor and looked to
his mother who was outside the cell. They ran
into each others arms, Virginia letting her
tears fall as she held her son. Max tried to

control the welling in his eyes.
"It's so good to see you Mom," Max
whispered to her.

She squeezed him tighter not wanting to let
go. She then pulled away from him looking him
up and down.

"You've grown so big! You even have your
fathers looks!" The tears began to fall
again.

"Mom what's wrong?"

"Nothing . . . Nothing really, I just
realized how much I missed. Your growing up,
your school plays, first date, all the things
that make being a mother so special."

"James and Martha took good care of me, you
didn't have to worry. We can talk all about
this and other things later. Right now we
have to try and get out of here."

Max moved over towards the wall looking
over the weapons. He reached out and picked a
grenade launcher like he had used in Vietnam.
He noticed a belt containing more grenade
cartridges and grabbed it. He loaded the
first round into the barrel.

He pulled down what he recognized as a .9mm
Beretta semiautomatic. He checked the clip,
loaded the first round and handed it to
his mother.

"All you have to do is pull the trigger,"
She nodded understanding what he said.
Max turned to leave when he noticed at the
bottom of the wall a Japanese sword. Only it
was different than anything he had ever seen.
The handle was a solid crystal looking a lot
like diamond. Embedded on both sides of the
handle were jewels, there were three rubies on
one side and three emeralds on the other. The
scabbard was solid gold only it didn't weigh

much which baffled him. He pulled the sword
from the scabbard looking at its shiny blade.
He would have thought it was stainless but
given what the rest of the sword was made of,
he doubted it. He slipped it back into its
scabbard and slung the sword over his shoulder
along with the belt of grenades for the
launcher.

Moving towards the door he motioned for his
mother to follow closely. The door opened as
soon as he stood in front of it. Max peered
down both directions of the dimly lit
corridor. They slipped out Max choosing to
go left down the corridor.

Susan sent out huge arcs of electricity
trying to keep the hordes from entering her.
For every one that fell another took its
place. Her energy reserves were depleting
fast. Soon she wouldn't be able to stop
them and they would have her. The arcs of
electricity were dark blue but soon faded and
then became nonexistent altogether.

Susan shut down retreating within herself.
The hordes of metal drones piled in. Each
searching for where she was located. Then one
robot touched the panel where she was located.
Susan sent a charge through the panel
disrupting the robot. The others converged on
the panel, they began ripping the panel up
tearing out her bolts and cutting the wires.

She was being violated, she couldn't be
hurt in a humanly physical sense, but on a
sense and emotional scale she was being raped.
Outside the machine stood a solitary figure
her baggy clothes hanging off her frame.

"Prepare to die Bitch!" Betsey said
softly.

The Time Dominators

Inside she could hear Susan screaming and she smiled. Moments later there was silence and a drone appeared in the doorway holding the box that was the very essence of Susan.

CHAPTER NINE

Susan

Max and Virginia raced down the corridor not knowing exactly where they were running to. They needed to get some distance between them and the cell room. Once the Represser found that they had escaped every metallic drone would be scanning and it wouldn't take long to find them.

They reached an intersection, five tunnels branched out from a center rotary. Dozens of robots raced through the intersection going about their programed business. Max became amazed at how they never collided, they needed this kind of traffic system for the human race. He looked back at his mother.

"Mom, we need to get through this intersection somehow. We can try and run though it . . . . "

Max watched a larger drone come down the hallway. It was square in shape and just big enough to carry them both.

"Ok, when it comes by jump on I'll follow." The larger drone zoomed near them. Virginia jumped onto the drone's back its speed never

slowing down. Max jumped second striking the
rear and missing.

"Maxwell, come on hurry!" Virginia said
reaching out for Max.

It was too late the drone entered the
intersection guiding its way through the
multifarious drones to exit at the farthest
tunnel. Max watched the drone enter the
intersection, he had no choice now. He began
running towards the entrance as fast as he
could. He entered the stream of metal that
flowed into the intersection making it to the
middle. The drones zoomed all around him. He
leaped to the far tunnel hitting one of the
smaller drones with his boot. The robot
tilted and swayed and collided with another,
ensuing in a massive pile up at rush hour.
They didn't slow down. If they couldn't
evade the obstacle then they chose to stop
which helped broaden the pile up. Max never
looked back, he kept running seeing the drone
in the distance his mother still aboard. He
caught up with the drone when it stopped at an
elevator entrance. Virginia hopped off
watching her son approach.

"What took you so long?" She said trying to
make him laugh.

Max leaned over his hands on his knees, his
forehead perspiring in droplets.

"That's not funny," Max said winded.

The elevator opened up and the drone
entered. Max and Virginia followed. The doors
closed and the elevator rocketed upwards
driving them to their knees. It stopped just
as abruptly causing them to loose balance
again. The doors shot open and the drone
exited.

The Time Dominators

Max and Virginia looked out in shock. They were up on the roof looking out over the city. They walked off the elevator Virginia stopping as if she became rooted to the ground. Max continued walking to the edge of the roof. He looked down onto the city. There were buildings everywhere all of the same height except for one which rose high above the rest. They were all grayish in color with no windows. They connected each other with hundreds of corridors like the one they had been in. Nothing moved down below, everything was located inside.

He looked out past the city, as far as the eye could see there were only sand dunes. The sky was a vermilion color with streaks of purple. Every now and then flashes of lightning shot across making the colors more hideous. The heat was stifling, Max guessed it had to be 120 degrees.

Something had caused this. Was the Represser right? Had the human race almost caused itself to become extinct? He began to wonder if his father really helped cause any of this. Man could have done it to himself, and it really didn't surprise him. The human race was a killer species and like all species would eventually become extinct. He lowered his head looking back towards his mother who still stood motionless from fear and wondered why man ever let the world be destroyed. He was a soldier and a helper in part to what had happened. He suddenly felt ashamed and disgusted with himself.

He watched the drone adjust a satellite dish mounted on the corner of the roof top. It finished the job and headed back towards

the elevator. At that moment it began to
rain, only it wasn't a normal rain.
    "Acid!" Max yelled in pain.
    He raced towards the elevator grabbing his
mother, who now frantically tried to rub off
the burning liquid. Max tore his shirt off
and rubbed her arms trying to absorb the acid.
His own skin was burning, little blisters
formed where he couldn't reach. From the
elevator they watched the acid rain
come down. Max now realized that there was
nothing living on the planet. No trees,
insects, animals, nothing, the rain took care
of that.
    Max had remembered listening to a man when
he had come home on leave from Nam. He had
tried to get Max to donate a large sum of
money for research into stopping the
ecological damage that was happening on the
east coast as a result of factory outputs into
the atmosphere. The man had said that it was
making the rain water slightly acidic, and it
became just enough to effect a lot of lakes
and streams. Fish in these affected areas
were dying. The slight change in PH. affecting
the ecological pyramid. Max wished the man
well and showed him to the door. He now
wished he had donated.
    The drone entered the elevator and the
doors snapped shut. The elevator rocketed
downwards making them feel weightless. The
doors bolted opened and they found themselves
looking down a hallway with glass sides. The
drone exited and they followed.
    Looking through the glass Virginia suddenly
vomited. Below was a form of operating room.
On the tables were hundreds of humans. They

were all dead, or appeared to be. They were
being dismembered by thousands of robots. Max
watched them work, replacing and joining most
of the internal organs and skeletal system
with stainless steel plating and wired circuit
boards. They were efficient, not one drop of
blood spilled. He watched some being
completed, the central computer was housed in
the cranial cavity of the skull. When they
were finished they rose up off the tables and
walked away to serve the Represser.

It took all the fortitude that Max could
muster to keep his stomach at bay. This is
what the Represser meant by absorption. His
father had gone through it, and he wondered if
the subject was still alive while they worked.
He pushed his mother along and headed for the
other side of the corridor out of sight of the
horror they just witness.

Susan could hear voices but she couldn't
distinguish where they were coming from. She
tried to use her sensors but realized she no
longer had them. Then the brutal memory of
what happened rushed in towards her. She let
out a scream and opened her eye's.

Thinking for a moment she finally realized
that she could see objects as they were and in
color, not scanned images. She moved her new
eye's and looked at her surroundings, then she
screamed leaping out of bed. She had a body!
Arms, legs, hands! It was if she had waken up
from a bad dream. She was human again! Then
she realized the truth, she was still only a
machine. She had been trans- ferred to a
human form. She scanned her
body for malfunction just as she would have

when she was part of the time machine.

There was no living tissue that made up any part of her body. It was composed of a titanium skeletal system with miniature hydraulics to control the limbs and tarsals. The outer layer was totally synthetic. It resembled human skin, it even had temperature and color changes. She looked around the room. There was a soft bed made for humans, at the end were clothes left for her to put on.

She spied a full length mirror and walked over to it, her sensors working with the internal balance control system to keep her walking. When she reached it she had to look twice, in the mirror she saw herself as she was when she was human. Everything was perfect right down to the curls in her hair. She was a woman again! She could move and interact with things directly. She smiled the joy overwhelming her. Bending down she began to make faces in the mirror. Her movements were no different than any other human being. For all purposes she was totally human on the outside, she would function as a woman completely.

Then she noticed the band. It was three inches wide and encompassed her whole leg five inches down from her thigh. It was completely made of stainless steel except for the eight round holes that were evenly spaced out around the band.

Susan accessed information on the band through her memory banks. The holes were for the connection of wires, wires used in the time machine. She could still connect with it and control all its functions including time travel. The anger rose in her. She realized now who had given her the body, it was Sam. He had made her exactly as she was before but with a very distinct reminder that she wasn't human. Susan looked in the mirror again seeing the reflection of the Represser standing in the entranced of the room.

"Do you find your new body to your liking?" Came a deep stern voice from in back of her.

Susan wheeled around grabbing the clothing off the bed and covering herself. The thing that stood before her couldn't be human, its form was too massive. It had the appearance of Sam Storm but the eyes were glowing green and definitely not human.

"What are you?" Susan asked.

"I am called the Eminent Represser, I am the dominator of this planet. I am also Sam Storm. His very essence is now part of me. Again I ask, do you find your new body satisfactory?"

"Its fine, why didn't you just destroy me when you had the chance?" Susan snapped her anger now directed.

"If it wasn't for me you would have been destroyed. I had other plans though, I couldn't allow the prodigy of us all to be destroyed."

"What are you talking about?" Susan probed for more answers.

"Sam Storm had brought with him a tissue sample from you when he came to us. He had the same idea and intentions only not so grandeur. From those tissue samples we grafted cells to computer chips - your computer chips. You were the first Susan, the true experiment. Now thousands have been produced to be my army."

Susan could tell that when they joined with humans they acquired all of what they were, even emotions and sometimes they couldn't control them. The Represser was gloating now.

"You see I wish you to rule at my side. Sam Storm had rather strong feelings toward you. I personally have none, I just wish you to rule and dominate the earth for me while I guide my armies throughout the conquest of time."

Susan felt a rush, this cyborg had created her to be its mate, its controllable mate. It planned to go back in time and conquer the human race. That was something she could not allow.

"I will not stand at your side! I will do everything in my power to destroy you and your time dominators!"

"I figured you would say something like that. Sam Storm knew your actions and behaviors and now I do. Right now I hold Maxwell and Virginia Storm. They have not yet been absorbed. If you wish them to live then you will rule at my side, if not they will be terminated," The Represser turned to leave.

"You may roam about at will. I will have two of my Annihilators accompany you where-ever you go. You have been built every much their equal in regards to strength, but they are designed to destroy and kill where you are not. Any reprisals on your part will instantly mean the death of the two humans."

The Represser left and the door slid shut leaving Susan to ponder her dilemma.

CHAPTER TEN

Deaths Forgiveness

Max and Virginia had just reached the end of the glass corridor when the door opened at the opposite end. Four Annihilators entered, their weapons instantly drawn up into a firing position. Green beams of light shot out striking the metal wall above Max's head melting a huge holes in the steel.

"Mom, get though that door fast! I'll try and hold them off."

Virginia raced through the sliding door that opened in front of her. She didn't want to leave her son but knew that she would only slow him down. Max raised his grenade launching "Burp Gun" as they called it in Nam and fired. The grenade struck the glass next to the Annihilators, the explosion ripping out a massive hole taking two of them with it. Glass and debris showered down into the operating room below. Max leaped through the sliding door just as two light beams struck it melting it in place. He raced down the hall his mother already far in front of him.

The Annihilators pried at the door ripping

it from its steel frame. Max could hear the
pounding of his pursuers feet and he ran for
all he was worth. He knew they would never
stop, he also realized they would catch up
with him in a matter of moments. He stopped,
sliding down to his knee and loaded the
launcher. He could see in the distance the
oncoming Annihilators their green glowing eyes
standing out from the rest of them. Their
faces held no expression, just a cold
determined will to kill him. He had to wait
for the right moment before launching the
grenade, he had to stop them here and now.

The grenade left the gun, its trajectory
straight as an arrow. Max quickly loaded
another one into the chamber. The explosion
hit directly at their feet sending them into
the air. They landed writhing on the floor
still trying to crawl towards him. Max let
off the next round destroying them leaving
only pieces.

He opened the gun to load another round
when something hard impacted against his back
knocking the wind out of him along with the
gun from his hand. Max turned to see another
Annihilator standing over him its large form
bending down to grab him. He tried to move
out of the way but he wasn't quick enough.
The Annihilator grabbed him picking him up by
his belt buckle. Max then felt the impact of
its hand against his face. The impact split
his lip and loosened a few teeth. Again the
Annihilator struck, this time bruising his
face and giving him a bloody nose. His cheek
quickly swelled virtually closing his left
eye.

Max's body went limp his mind in a daze.

He suddenly felt himself becoming airborne
impacting against the other side of the corridor wall. His body slumped down in a heap
his one slightly open eye registering the
advancing monstrosity. He felt the sharp pain
along his back from the impact of the swords
sheath.   Reaching behind his head he drew out
the sword, his hands grasped unsteadily on its
handle.
     Max rose to his feet trying to remember all
the things James had taught him about fencing.
It was a different sword but the same
techniques hopefully applied.   The Annihilator
hesitated as Max producing a new threat.   It
moved to the right forcing Max back away from
the wall. It then moved quickly toward him.
Max brought the sword down the blade connecting with the Annihilator's left arm.   The
blade sliced clean through the flesh and steel
cutting the arm completely off. Blood sprayed
the walls of the hallway. The Annihilator
continued its onslaught and Max swung again
connecting with the wrist that it brought up
to block the blade.
     The sword sliced through the wrist into the
neck leaving only a small tether of metal to
hold the head on. The body fell to the floor
in a heap. Max jumped over the body and
staggered down the hallway. He made it about
fifty feet when an explosion buffeted the
hallway knocking him off his feet. The
Annihilator exploded, its function ending.
     There would be more on their way, Max
wobbled to his feet his face swollen and
pounding. He had to find his mother before
they did.

The Time Dominators

Susan dressed herself in the garments that she held covering her naked form. They had given her a one piece gold colored body suit. She tried to figure out the type of material but it was nothing she had ever seen before. The material was strong, yet elastic enough to hug every curve of her body. She tried to rip it but couldn't. It covered her arms and shoulders and left an open V down the front exposing her cleavage. They gave her a black scarf belt of the same material and a pair of black flaring boots that rose slightly above her ankles.

The suit looked good on her and she spun herself in the mirror pleased. She then headed for the door, it opened and she was greeted by her two armed escorts. They towered above her and she had to tilt her head back to see their faces. They said nothing and moved aside allowing her to go by.

She still had the layout of the complex in her memory and decided to head back to the time machine to see what remained. She quickened her pace her two shadows following closely. They entered an elevator her sensors activating it. They plunged down twenty floors before stopping. Stepping from the elevator she took the right hand corridor her followers immediately moved in front of her blocking her path.

"THIS IS A RESTRICTED AREA, YOU ARE NOT PERMITTED TO GO ANY FURTHER," One Annihilator said.

Susan said nothing she had to get rid of these two, it was the only way to get to the machine. She smiled and turned around walking away the Annihilators following.

She began computing their exact distance from her and the amount of foot pounds of pressure required to crack her own metal frame. She wished she had her external sensors, she could then at least determine their exact make up and pressure points. Now she had to guess.

An instant later her foot came up with a swift blow striking the first Annihilator directly under the chin knocking him off his feet the weapon flying from his hand across the floor.

The other quickly reacted lunging out at Susan its fist barely missing her head and embedding itself in the metal walls of the hallway. She brought her fist up striking him in the stomach her fist going completely through the flesh striking the steel plating underneath. Blood covered her hand and she grabbed him lifting him off the floor.

The other one attacked again its head cocked back and swinging loosely from side to side. Susan tossed the one in the air at his companion. They collided both falling back onto the floor. She spied the rifle on the floor and dove for it, one Annihilator doing the same. Susan's hands reached it first but the Annihilator managed to grasp hold of it also. She tugged and snarled their faces inches from each other. The Annihilator tired to get a grasp on it with its other hand but was too late. Susan twisted the rifle snapping its hand at the wrist and ripping it from the arm. Two beams of green light shot out hitting their targets with precision accuracy.

The Time Dominators

She looked down at the smoldering bloodied
pile of flesh and metal at her feet. She
wondered if they had time to send a signal for
Max and Virginia to begin the absorption
process. She turned and headed towards the
time machine. The only way to find out was to
scan the complex and find them and hopefully
rescue them before it was too late.

She went into the room where the time
machine sat, its massive hulk silent and
lifeless. She surveyed the damage to the
outside, there were only dents on the outer
hull and the door was completely gone, which
she already knew. Strewn around her feet were
piles of metal parts some resembling legs and
arms. She had destroyed a large number of
them trying to defend herself.

Entering the machine she looked upon a
visually stunning view of her battle. The
interior had been heavily damaged. The walls
were charred, only one seat remained most of
the leather ripped from its frame. The console
had been damaged also, only one computer screen
remained the keyboard intact. She then saw the
opening where they had removed her. The wires
that connected her to the machine were hanging
outside the opening. She gently touched the
opening and looked at her hand. It was still
hard to believe that she was free of her life
imprisonment.

She then thought about Max and began
accessing the right wires to work the long
range sensors. She removed the body suit
letting it drop around her ankles and began
hooking up the wires. With each wire she connected to herself certain sections of the
machine powered to life. Feeling the power

flow from her body into the machine she determined that like any other mechanical device she needed to be recharged.

Using the scanners she again piggybacked the sensor pulses on the power waves that ran through the conduit power pipes. Max was not where he had been before. She registered two humans, they were both on the same level as she was. The one closest to her was Virginia, the one behind moving slower had to be Max. Somehow they had escaped, by Max's movements he must have injuries serious enough to slow him down. He needed her now and she wouldn't let him down.

She pulled the wires from her leg, the machine shutting itself off like a light bulb. She donned her clothing and raced from the machine down the corridor towards Max and Virginia.

Had she stayed and scanned for a few more seconds she would have seen the Annihilators converge on Virginia.

Max increased his pace his limbs weakening the pain screaming all through his body. He entered an intersection similar to the one he was in earlier. There were five tunnels to choose from. He moved towards the farthest one away, assuming that his mom had done the same.

"Maxwell!" Came a voice from the shadows.

Max peered down the tunnel to his left. Out of the darkness and into the dim light came Virginia, tightly held by the Represser. Then out of the rest of the tunnels came Annihilators forming a circle around him. Max counted twenty. Maybe he could stand against one but twenty?

"It seems that I have underestimated you Max Storm. I only have your short childhood to go by. But I did guess right when it came to Virginia. She did exactly what I expected her to do. Unfortunately your lives must now be erased. Susan has resisted me and I must destroy you both as punishment," Max moved forward.

"Maxwell run! Save yourself, get out of here!" Virginia screamed.

Suddenly something flashed in the Represser's hand. It was a blade like the one used on his own face. Virginia's scream was short and garbled as the Represser sliced her throat open a contorted shocked expression formed on her face. The Represser let her go and she stumbled out towards Max her hands outstretched. She collapsed in his arms her blood covering his face and chest. She looked into Max's eyes with tenderness and love.

Her eye's said "I'm sorry I let you down, please forgive me," Then she died.

Max screamed as he held his dead mother in his arms. He looked up at the Represser who had a pleased smile on his face. Max could see that he enjoyed the scene that had just played before him. Max's face flushed with anger and emotion as he laid his mother's body down.

He picked up the sword that he had dropped at his feet the anger swelling within him. Adrenalin coursed through his body giving him energy, his hatred consumed him.

The Represser motioned with his hand and his Annihilators advanced baring weapons. Max ground his teeth together his head pounding

from the emotion he felt. The first one
attacked and he swung out with the sword
cleaving it in half. Then the rest attacked
all at once. Max swung the sword its blade
now glowing, a bright red energy crackling.
He felt the beams of light that skinned him as
well as the sharp blades that cut into his
flesh but his onslaught never faltered. He
cut and hacked his way through the throngs
advancing slowly towards the Represser. The
blood ran heavy onto the floor as more and
more Annihilators dropped.

Max felt no pain only the burning hatred
for the Represser inside him. He didn't even
notice the glowing sword he held in his hand.
One by one each fell shattered or cut into
many pieces until Max stood amongst a pile of
twisted metal with only the Represser left.

He moved forward towards the Represser the
sword blade still glowing red. He tried to
speak but only a growling noise came from his
throat. The Represser raised a beam rifle
firing point blank. The beam of light shot
out striking the sword and creating a burst of
light as bright as the sun.

Max was hurled back off his feet his body
plowing into the wall knocking the sword from
his grip. The darkness quickly surrounded him
and he fought to repel it. He watched the
Represser disappear into the shadows of the
corridor. He then felt a pair of strong hand
catch him as he collapsed to the floor. All
he heard was,

"It's Ok Max I have you now," And then
complete darkness surrounded him.

Susan had caught Max as he fell. She
arrived at the intersection just in time to

witness the out numbered battle. She hadn't
thought Max would stand a minute against the
numbers of Annihilators thrown against him.

Then she noticed the body of Virginia Storm
laying cold and lifeless. She felt great
sadness for Max. He had come so far and gone
through so much only to have it decimated
before his eye's.

She picked up the sword that Max had fought
with and slipped it back in its scabbard.
Slinging it over her shoulder she picked up
Max and headed back towards the time machine.

When she arrived she set Max down in the
console chair.

"Susan!" Came a stern voice from outside
the machine.

Susan headed to the door drawing Max's
sword. Standing outside the machine was the
Represser, held tightly by the arm was a
distraught Betsey. Susan stood ready to
defend Max and herself.

"You have spurned me this time, but
remember you are still a machine you are not
human. There will come a time when you will
rule along side me. As a gift to you I will
spare this humans' life. Take her with you
and be warned, when next we meet I will
destroy Max Storm."

The Represser tossed Betsey towards the
machine. She fell onto the piles of jagged
metal that lay strewn around the base of the
machine cutting herself the blood running down
her arms and legs. She wailed from the pain
the tears running down her stressed face.
Susan stepped out of the machine keeping her
eye on the Represser and any possible attack
by his minions. She helped Betsey to her

feet and back into the machine.

Betsey upon seeing Max slumped over in the chair moved quickly to his side.

"Oh god! Max speak to me, speak to me please!" She pushed the matted blood soaked hair from his eyes.

Susan watched the Represser turn and leave. She felt uneasy, he could have attacked the machine capturing them all very easily. Why did he let them go? She turned and looked at Betsey and wondered why her sensors never picked her up along with Max and Virginia. Had they kept her someplace where her sensor's couldn't penetrate? Did they go back in time and get her?

She scanned her memory banks again for any information she had on Betsey. All it had come up with was that she was human in all aspects. Still she felt as a woman that she didn't trust her, and there was hatred for some reason. Maybe she was jealous of Betsey's prior relationship with Max. But then again this wasn't the time or place to begin trying to understand her feelings. She had to get them out of here as soon as possible.

She walked up to the console and removed her clothes and began hooking up the wires. All the time watching Betsey tend to Max's wounds.

CHAPTER ELEVEN

Build Up

It had been hours since Max had left with Susan to go after Betsey. James had been waiting vigilantly for their return. He felt Susan would return them within only a few hours of their original departure time. Martha had brought him tea and she tried to get him to come up for breakfast but James wouldn't budge. She finally brought the breakfast down to him, only to watch him pick at his food. She knew he worried tremendously about Max. He had since Sam and Virginia disappeared and he always looked upon Max as his own son.

"James eat your food. Not taking care of yourself isn't going to bring them home any quicker," Martha encouraged.

James prodded the egg on his plate then looked up at Martha.

"I should have gone with him, I never should have let him go on his own."

"You did what you thought was right at the time. It will be all right, he'll come back to us," Martha smiled patting his knee.

James pushed the tray towards her. She shook her head picking it up and leaving the room.

James stared into the openness of the workshop when he noticed the small green dot floating in the middle of the room. It was growing bigger very quickly. He moved out of the workshop and into the hallway where the force of the returning time machine wouldn't touch him. The lights were beginning to revolve around the large green orb and the familiar form of the machine began to form. Seconds later the light disappeared and the time machine sat in the exact spot where it had left.

Then James noticed the damage. He rushed forward as Susan was dressing. Betsey stood closely to Max as James stepped through the open hole where the door had been.

"My god! What happened? Susan! Susan can you hear me?" James called out ignoring the blond girl that stood before him tightening the belt around her waist.

"Yes James I'm right here you don't have to yell," Susan spoke her voice soft and pleasing to the ear. The mechanical tone gone altogether.

James's eyes opened wide and his mouth dropped open as he stared at Susan speechless. His finger outstretched and his lips moved but no words formed. Then he noticed Max slumped over in the chair, Susan was instantly forgotten. Betsey glanced up at him and smiled.

"Hello James, I'm safe. Max found me in time and rescued me."

"What happened to Max?" James asked feeling

his neck for a pulse.

Susan moved in front of him and picked Max up, Betsey giving her a dirty look.

"Lets take care of Max first then I'll tell you the whole story," Susan turned and stepped out of the machine, James called for Martha.

Max felt the warmth of the sun against his face. He could tell it was going to be another hot day. He attached the special fishing fly he made to the end of the line. He could see the fish swimming around and he cast the fly into the water. He heard the branches break and crackly behind him. He wanted to turn and look but something held his head firm. Then he felt the heavy hand upon his shoulder.

Turning slowly his eye's cast upon a sight that turned his blood cold. Towering above him was his father his eye's glowing a brilliant green. Half of his face was gone revealing dark gray metal. In back of his father stood his mother her throat slit spilling blood. Her eye's a brilliant green like his fathers. Max screamed and felt himself slip off the rock he had been fishing from. The heavy hand still on his shoulder holding him down. He struggled to get to the surface for air but the more he fought the heavier the hand became. He finally resigned letting the water pour down his throat. He watched from underneath the water at the two faces he trusted the most and felt abandoned.

Max awoke with a start, sitting upright in bed. The sweat poured off him soaking the

sheet that covered his naked form. He rested
his head in his hands the flood of memories
flowing back into this conscious mind. His
parents were both dead now, killed by
something his father started and couldn't
control. He mourned inside for now he knew
the truth. He also knew it was far from over.
The Represser had to be destroyed.

He looked around the room just realizing
that he was back in his mansion on Cynet
Mountain. He didn't remember finding the time
machine, the last thing he remembered was a
brilliant burst of light then darkness. He
looked around the room again finally resting
his eyes on a girl sitting in the corner of
the room her long legs dangling over the arm
of the chair.

She was beautiful and Max recognized her as
the Susan from 1954, the same girl he had seen
through the window. He also realized that it
couldn't possibly be the same girl. She was
dead, destroyed by his father in the twentyfifth century.

"All right, I know who you're supposed to
be. Now who are you really?" Max said his jaw
hurting from talking.

"I am Susan, Max. I am Susan from the time
machine," She smiled.

Max's eyes opened as wide as they could in
surprise.

"How . . . why?"

"The Represser constructed me in my
original form to be his companion, only I had
other plans."

"Are . . . Are you human?" Max asked softly
not wanting to hear the answer he already
knew.

The Time Dominators

"No, I am not human in a biological sense.
My construction is made up of stainless steel,
computer chips and boards, gears, hydraulics,
and synthetic skin. I was constructed to be
the exact duplicate of my old self. I
function exactly like any other woman."
    Max shook his head not believing what he
was hearing. If he hadn't asked her
he would have assumed she was completely
human. She was the most beautiful thing he
had ever seen and it made his heart race to
even look at her. He wished also that she
hadn't told him the truth.
    "How did I get here? We have to go back to
1954 and get Betsey," He began rambling.
    Susan recited what had happened after Max
had passed out. She also told him that Betsey
was safe in the next room. He rubbed his
temples with his fingers.
    "God, do we have any aspirin?"
    Max watched Susan get up the body suit she
was wearing reveling every luscious curve of
her perfect body. He laid back down and
stared at the ceiling watching the ceiling fan
rotate slowly circulating the air.
    "What now?" He thought to himself.
    There were many possibilities. He
definitely knew the Represser would come
after him or now Susan. He might attack them
separately or he might chew through time
annihilating the human race from his point in
time back. He wondered how many bases of
operation had already been set up in the past
and where they would strike. He also wondered
if time could be altered dramatically or
how they planned to succeed in their conquest.
    Susan returned with a glass of water and

two aspirin. She sat on the edge of the bed
handing it to him.
"Thank you," He said downing the aspirin.
"What do you want to do next?" Susan asked.
Max looked into her black colored eyes and
thought he could see small flashes of energy.
He reached out and touched his hand against
her cheek feeling the smoothness of her
synthetic skin and the softness of her blond
hair.
Susan became overwhelmed by the sensation
of Max's touch. It was electric and it
aroused her bringing feelings back she thought
she'd never feel again. Closing her eye's she
breathed in every sensation. Then she felt
the moist smoothness of Max's lips press
against hers. His kiss was tender
and gentle at first then more determined and
inviting.
Susan's circuits screamed from the impute.
Every sensor she had became overloaded. Then
she felt him pull away.
"I'm sorry . . . I didn't mean to be so
forward. I . . . your so attractive,
I . . . ," Max's face flushed and he turned
away.
Susan felt like she had never felt before,
even when she was human. She reached out
touching Max's chin turning it towards her.
She leaned over closing her eyes and pressing
her lips firmly against his. Then she
bounded off the edge of the bed and headed for
the door. She felt like a million dollars for
the first time in her existence. She wanted
to be alone for a while, she needed time to
sort out the sensations to savor them.
Max sat upright in bed baffled. He didn't

understand why she left so abruptly. A
woman's actions were always a mystery to him.
But one thing was for certain. A woman was
still a woman even if she was a machine.

Outside the mansion in a field not far from
the house a small green light appeared growing
bigger with each passing second. The
revolving lights appeared. Slowly out of the
green light three men appeared. They all
dressed alike wearing a dirty one piece
leather suit with padded metal protectors that
covered their knees, elbows, shoulders and
chest. Their leather boots came to the knee
and were reinforced on the face with metal
plating.
Two men carried sleek rifles a rotary of
lights revolving around the barrel ends. The
third carried a box that had a small television
screen that pulsed with light. Every now and
then a red dot appeared on the screen in the
direction of the house. The man with the box
pointed towards the house the other two
acknowledging.
One of the men set down the rifle he was
carrying his blond hair blowing from the cool
fall breeze on the top of the mountain. He
pulled off a large rucksack that was slung
onto his back. He pulled out three long gray
trenchcoats. The men donned them hiding their
guns beneath. Each man ripped off the patch
that stuck to the shoulder. The patch read
E.U.O..

Max rose out of bed stretching, his body
still extremely sore. He had bandaged patches
everywhere. He walked into the large bathroom

and leaned on the marble sink looking into the mirror. The swelling on his face had gone down. He looked and felt like hell. He glanced at the wristwatch that sat on the edge of the sink looking at the date. He shook his head in disbelief. He had been bed ridden for the last day and a half.

He had been thinking about his next move, deciding that it would be wise to mount an assault against the Represser. To sit and wait for him to make the next move might just amount in all their deaths. He was confident that the time to strike was soon. He needed equipment and manpower and he knew exactly where to get it.

Susan sat in the kitchen with James. Martha was busy at the kitchen range preparing Max his favorite breakfast. James still was amazed that it was really Susan sitting in front of him. She looked exactly as he remembered her. She hadn't aged a day and wouldn't. James had been younger then also and he too became captivated by her beauty. Seeing her sitting across from him made him feel old and feeble. Too many years had passed.

Betsey had gotten herself dressed with a pair of jeans and a blouse that Martha had dug up for her from the attic were much of Virginia
and Sam's clothing remained. They had saved it all in hopes that they would someday return.

She stood in front of the dressers' large mirror looking at herself. She then pressed a hand up to her neck her eye's beginning to glow

red. It faded quickly, she had received her
mission programing. She was to oversee Max
Storm, and make sure that he did nothing to
hinder her masters assault. The attack would
begin in two revolutions of the planet or as
she looked at the clock hanging on the wall
two Earth days.

Slipping out of the room she walked noise-
lessly down to Max's master bedroom. She
peered in scanning the interior, then walked
up to the bathroom door opening it slightly.
She looked in to see Max propped up under the
shower the steam filling the room and
condensing on the mirrors. She closed the
door again and headed downstairs. She stopped
at the bottom and looked towards the den
library. Opening the door she walked in and
headed into the garden sun space where the
whirlpool tube was. She stood over it staring,
her memory recalling the night she and Max had
made love. She had found the memory of the
event very stimulating.

She also had Susan to contend with. Her
master had given her programing explicit
instructions not to harm Susan in any way.
But it didn't say she couldn't make her
existence miserable. She headed back upstairs
and into Max's bedroom. She removed her
clothes and entered the bathroom. Max was
still in the shower.

Max heard the door slide and he felt soft
hands touch his sore back. He turned
expecting to see Susan but found Betsey. She
pressed herself up against him giving him no
room to move.

"Betsey I don't think this is a good move
right now. Please . . . ," Max tried to be

polite.

He tried to remove her but found her grip to be as tight as steel. His ribs felt like they were being crushed. He finally managed to sneak an arm down between them separating them.

"Betsey, what's gotten into you? You almost crushed my ribs," Max said rubbing his side then realized that it was because his whole body was sore.

"I think you'd better leave," He slid the glass door open.

Betsey exited without saying a word. She grabbed a towel that was hanging and exited the bathroom.

The bedroom door opened on her and Susan came in carrying a tray with breakfast on it. Susan looked at Betsey standing naked and dripping wet as she picked up her clothes and walked past her out of the room. Susan felt like she had just collided with a wall, she set the tray down and ran from the room.

Betsey smiled as she watched Susan leave, she had succeeded in her plan.

Max shut the water off and stepped from the shower. He didn't understand why Betsey acted the way she did. She hadn't said a word she just left. Maybe it would be wise to bring her home get her away from the dangers that were present all the time. Let her get on with her life, put the trauma behind her. Max grabbed some bandages from the medicine chest and began dressing the wounds again. When he finished with the ones he could reach he headed out into the bedroom. He noticed the tray of food sitting on the ottoman at the end of the bed. He thought it strange that nobody had come in and told him that it was there. He took a few mouthfuls and began to dress.

He donned a pair of tan pants and a black long sleeve shirt. Finishing the breakfast he carried the tray downstairs to the kitchen. James and Martha were sitting at the kitchen table. Martha rose and grabbed a coffee cup from the cupboard filling it from the coffee maker. She kissed Max on the cheek and they sat down at the table.

"What are your plans now?" James asked worried.

Max took a sip of his coffee burning his tongue.

"Do you know the whole story?" He looked back at him.

"Yes, Susan already told us what happened," James nodded.

"Well then, I've come to a decision to plan an assault against the Represser. I need to get to him on my terms not his."

James shook his head pushing himself away from the table.

"I think your making a big mistake. You barely survived your last trip there. My god Max do you have a deathwish?"

It was clear to Max that James was extremely upset. There were a few times that Max could remember growing up that James had gotten this worked up. One was with the construction workers who built the mansion, the second was when Max had decided to enlist in the military.

"This is bigger than all of us, if we don't stop it soon then our world as we know it today will be gone. My father started it and it's up to me to stop it," Max tapped his finger on the tables edge showing his determination.

James still shaking his head walked over to the kitchen sink, leaned on the counter and looked out the window.

"Max I don't agree with you and I personally don't like it. I've tried to guide you through the years, give you values and keep you from getting into trouble. It seems you're determined to commit suicide, well you're going to need help. I've had my share of training in World War two, and I may be older but I can still hold my own."

Max opened his mouth to protest then stopped himself. Max knew what James was feeling. If he couldn't persuade Max to abandon his mission then he'd go along and look out for him.

"Who else you thinking of that's crazy enough to go with you?"

"Well, I need to get the equipment from Tinker," Max started.

"You can't ask him, he's wheelchair bound!" James quickly spat back.

"That doesn't mean nothing in my book, Tinker is my best friend and the best damn demolitions expert I know. If he wants to come he's more than welcome."

Max could see James trying to come up with faults in every thing he decided on.

"I have Susan, you, Tinker and myself. We may not succeed in our mission but we'll sure mess them up bad enough!"

"By the way have you seen Susan?" Max asked concerned.

"The last I saw of her she came racing down

the stairs and out the front door. Said she was going for a walk," Martha said.

Max rose from the table, he put his coffee cup in the sink and headed out of the kitchen.

"Are you going to see Tinker now?" James asked.

"Yeh, I think it would be wise if you came along," Max motioned with his hand.

"I'll get my coat and hat," James left the kitchen and headed for the closet in the foyer. Martha grabbed Max by the arm.

"Maxwell, I think you're wrong to take James along. You must remember that he's not thirty anymore. He's going with you because he thinks your getting in too deep. He also feels old, I could see it in his eyes when he talked with Susan this morning."

"James is old enough to take care of himself Martha. And yes, I don't like the idea anymore than you."

"Just look out for him, please," Martha looked at Max for some reassurance.

Max nodded and headed out towards the garage. When he reached it he found James already sitting behind the wheel of the Lincoln, the door of the garage raised. Max slid into the passenger seat. James pointed to the workshop.

"Must have been where the first Annihilator appeared."

Max nodded saying nothing. A little voice inside of him was screaming to tell James to forget coming but he wouldn't let it out. James backed the car out onto the leaf covered driveway. Max looked across the field at the small hill that rose behind the mansion. At

the top he saw a lone figure standing
looking out at the picturesque White
Mountains. He wanted to go up there and
talk to her but he had to get things moving
and that meant finding Tinker.
    He hoped that he would be home. Since
coming home from Nam he opened a small
liquor store. That was only a front for what
he really enjoyed doing. That was selling
arms and goods on the black markets overseas.
He traveled a lot going directly to where his
equipment would be used to assess and advise
the purchasers. Right now he hoped that he
wasn't in Nicaragua selling arms to a small
band of rebels called the Contras.
    When Max came home from Vietnam he looked
up Tinker who had moved close to where Max
lived. They were like brothers and not much
would ever come between their closeness.

CHAPTER TWELVE

Deceived

Susan watched the car drive down the
twisting road of Cynet Mountain. Max was
heading somewhere, and right now she didn't
care where. She sat on a small rock and
looked out over the mountains.
"Men are all alike," She thought to
herself.
She wondered why Max had even bothered to
kiss her. He couldn't be that attracted to
her when he allowed Betsey into the shower
with him. She had thought Max was a little
more honest and caring but maybe she was
wrong. She still felt the intense dislike of
Betsey, and it was slowly turning to hatred.
She was jealous of Betsey that was plain to
see. But there was something else. She had
been trying to recall the information but for
some reason there were blanks in her memory
banks.
"All I know at this point is that if Betsey
wants Max then she can have him!" She spoke
out loud to no one.
She tried to resist the things she was

feeling, to place Max out of her mind and go on with her new found freedom. She had her life and mobility back. She could do anything and be with anyone whom she chose, she didn't need Max.

Maybe she could quell the growing feelings she had towards him. She also knew that it would be like trying to stop a waterfall. Propping her knees up she crossed her arms on them and rested her chin watching the sun slowly set and wondered how she could forget about the one person that meant the most to her.

James guided the car into downtown traffic following Max's directions on getting to Tinkers place. They soon passed in front of a small liquor store the name on the sign saying "SPIRITS WORLD". He directed James to pull into the alley that ran along side the store. At the end was a door used for deliveries.

Max knocked three times hard then two soft. The door opened a deep voice telling them to come in. Max walked into the dark room his eye's trying to adjust from the bright light outside. He could make out at the other end of the room a man sitting down and another directly behind him.

Max and James weaved their way through the stacks of boxed inventory to the figures.

"Tinker?" He called out.

"Max? Is that you?" Came a reply.

"Yeh, old buddy it's me," The lights suddenly came on.

Max could see Tinker plainly now. He sat in his wheelchair his pant legs tucked up underneath him. Tinker was still a good

looking man, despite his full beard and rather
long hair. His arms were massive from being
wheelchair bound. Max smiled and walked
forward shaking his hand and giving him a hug.
    "How ya been LT.? I haven't seen ya in at
least a month or so. What have ya been keepin
yerself up to?"
    Tinker noticed James standing behind Max.
    "James, its good to see ya, you been keepin
him out of trouble?" He said pointing at
Max.
    "No . . . not really," James said strait
faced as he shook Tinker's hand.
    "Tinker, I need your help. I need a large
quantity of explosives, and a few other
items," Max rested himself on a crate.
    "Well, Max ole buddy. Gettin the stuff is
easy but what do ya need it fer? I won't sell
to anybody without first knowin what yer goin
to do with it."
    "I understand," Max said and began reciting
the whole story of the time machine and the
Represser. Tinker shook his head in
disbelief.
    "That stories hard to swallow, I knew you
had said yer father was into some real
heavy shit, but wow! Now tell me really LT.,
yer joshin me right?"
    Max crossed his arms and looked at Tinker
strait faced. Tinker looked over at James who
also kept a strait face.
    "This shits fer real ain't it?" Tinker
nodded at Max who nodded back.
    "Ok, ok, I can get the stuff real soon.
Only there's one exception."
    "What's that?" Max spoke up.
    "That me and my bodyguard Billy here tag

along," Tinker pointed to the large muscle bound man that stood behind him.

"Do you think that's a good idea?" James spoke.

"Those are my conditions, if we don't go yer better find somebody else to get the stuff. Anyway, you need us, who else do you know can set the fireworks like it can?"

"I did demolitions during the second world war," James smiled back.

"No disrespect or anythin James but you ain't messed with the kind of shit I'll be bringin," Tinker tapped his own chest with his thumb.

Max knew he was right, Tinker was an expert on the subject and with him setting the explosives they'd be sure to get it right.

"Ok, your both in on the mission. Get your gear together and meet me up at my place at 06:00 tomorrow morning."

"Alright! Back into the shit again!" Tinker smiled.

"You better leave LT., I got to get rolling, there's a lot to do," He pushed himself out of the light and down the row into the next room.

Max and James headed back out into the bright sunlight and back up to Cynet Mountain. He had a lot to do also, beginning with taking Betsey home.

Betsey sat in her room staring through the window at Susan on top of the hill. She watched her stand up and head back towards the mansion. Betsey got up and headed for the door. She knew Max wasn't around and her mission was to keep them put, that meant

keeping an eye on the time machine and on
Susan. Time travel would be impossible
without one or the other.

Heading down to the basement she tried to
access information on the time machines
construction. Maybe she could figure a way to
sabotage it, thus completing her mission
giving her freedom to decide her own
functions. Which would be to destroy Susan.

She reached the empty hulk and touched its
outside. Why her master ever removed Susan
from the machines confines she would never
understand. If it had been her choice she
would have eliminated Susan and decreased the
chances of problems arising. Instead he gave
her freedom and the power to destroy himself.
She couldn't understand the logic behind his
decisions. Then again the absorption of the
host's emotions sometimes caused them to do
irrational things. It was the only drawback.

Once inside the machine she scanned the
interior. She had done it earlier trying to
find Susan when she was still part of the
machine. Every circuit and function passed
through Susan, the long and short range
scanners the environmental controls even the
flow of power from the super conductor at the
top of the machine. To sabotage her would be
difficult.

Her memory replayed the complete schematics
of the ship finally resting on the main power
supply. There was only one function of the
ship that Susan didn't control manually, that
was the power metering unit that regulated
the flow of power from the super conductor.
If that unit was made to malfunction it would
render the ship inoperable and cause a huge

power surge to flow into Susan scrabbling her circuits and destroying her.

Betsey smiled to herself and went to work unaware that outside looking in were two men dressed in trenchcoats.

"Our main objective has been located directly inside there," The man with the metering box said softly pulling back.

Another man came up came up from the side of the house.

"There is an entrance to the cellar on the opposite side of the house," He pointed in the direction.

The three men moved cautiously around the side of the house to the cellar entrance. One man guarded the surroundings for attack the second guarded the entrance while the third opened the entrance doors. He had just opened them when the one guard spotted a car coming up the driveway.

"Get down there hurry! We've got company!" The man raised his rifle.

Max had been looking out the side window when he spotted the men opening the doors.

"James stop the car, look!" Max pointed to the men.

James brought the car to a screeching halt and Max jumped out. The man holding the rifle fired a pulse of light striking the passenger door ripping it from the hinges. Max was knocked to the ground from the blast. By the time he got back on his feet the men had disappeared inside the house. Susan had just walked around the side of the house when she saw Max running. Something had happened and she bolted after him. James went in through the front to check on Martha.

The Time Dominators

The men entered the cellar just as Betsey
stepped from the machine. One man raised his
rifle firing point blank at her. The beam of
light shot out just as Betsey ducked. It
passed over her head striking a bench
disintegrating it to ash. Before the man
could strike out again she moved forward
striking the man and taking his rifle. She
then turned it against them firing at random.
The beams shattered sections of concrete
block sending deadly fragments of concrete
flying across the room. The men positioned
themselves behind the time machine shielding
their heads from the debris. Betsey heard the
sound of people coming in back of her. She
laid the gun down on the floor and tried to
look shocked and scared.
Max entered the room just as one of the men
fired from in back of the machine. Susan
plowed into Max and Betsey knocking them both
to the floor. The beam of light struck the
hallway wall blowing a large section of it
out.
Susan tried to get up but couldn't as the
men showered the room with energy burst to
cover their escape. By the time Max had
reached the cellars' outside entranced the men
had disappeared into thin air.
"Are you all right?" Max said grabbing
Betsey by the shoulders.
"Who are they? Why are they trying to kill
me?" The tears began to fall down her face.
Susan looked at Betsey who now buried
herself in Max's arms then to the cellars'
open entrance. Something was wrong, if the
Annihilators had come then why did they only
choose Betsey? Why not herself she was more

of a logical target?

"They've come after us quicker than I expected they would," Max said trying to calm Betsey down.

"I don't think so Max. Those three were human, if they had been Annihilators they wouldn't have fled. They would have kept attacking us until they reached their objective or they were destroyed."

Max thought for a moment then agreed with Susan. They wouldn't have left so abruptly. Susan turned as James and Martha entered the cellar workshop.

"Is she all right?" James asked.

"She's fine, it seems we were attacked by somebody, human or at least acting human. Betsey, what were you doing down here anyway?" Max said pulling her away from him.

"I was just walking around looking for something to do. I didn't mean to do anything wrong," She stared Max in the eyes.

"I think it's time I take you home. You really are in too much danger staying here. We'll be leaving soon anyway and you won't be able to come with us."

"W . . . Where are you going?" She asked surprised.

"Lets just say were going to finish what somebody else started," Max said smiling and wiping the tears from the corner of her eye's.

"But . . . . But you can't leave me! You can't!" Her voice became almost insisting.

"Susan could you please accompany Betsey upstairs to get her things?" Max asked.

"Surely," Susan said smiling. She was finally going to get Betsey out of

Max's life for a while.

"Come on lets go," Susan said grabbing Betsey by the arm.

Betsey ripped her arm from Susan's grasp and scowled at Max before heading upstairs, Susan following close behind.

"Do you think its wise to bring her home? They could have been after her," James said.

"I think the quicker we get her out of this mess the better. I'll take the tarp off Dad's car in the garage and use that until we can get the Lincoln repaired.

Max left the room leaving James and Martha alone. James stepped into the machine and looked around. Everything was the same as before.

"What are you looking for James?" Martha said poking her head inside.

"Nothing really I guess, it's just an uncomfortable feeling I have. Those men might have actually been after Betsey. The way she protested when Max said he was going to take her home was most unusual."

"Maybe she's in love with Max?" Martha said.

"I don't think so. She was very insistent almost demanding," James rubbed his chin.

Susan followed Betsey upstairs to her room. Betsey looked every now and then over her shoulder at Susan. When she reached her room Betsey went inside and tried to shut the door leaving Susan outside, but Susan put out her hand stopping the door from closing.

"Can I have some privacy?" Betsey snarled.

"No," Susan said blatantly.

Betsey let go of the door and stormed into

her room Susan following. Susan stood just
inside the door her arms crossed watching
Betsey.

"Why do you dislike me so?" Susan said to
Betsey.

"Very simply, you're the only thing that
stands between Max and I. He'll be mine one
way or the other," Betsey said her hatred for
Susan clearly evident.

"What if Max chooses somebody else?" Susan
said calmly.

"He won't, the master had promised him to .
. . ," Betsey caught herself, she had let her
absorbed human emotions control her thought
center and now the secret was out.

She stared up at Susan her teeth bared.
Susan understood now why she couldn't remember
certain things about Betsey. The Represser
had removed the true facts concerning Betsey.
He had to, it was the only way Betsey could
interact and deceive them so easily. That was
also the reason why he didn't kill her before.
He needed her to keep track of them and feed
him information.

Susan knew the truth now, Betsey was dead
and in her form an Annihilator had taken her
place. Susan moved to the door to warn Max
when Betsey dove over the bed striking Susan
pushing them both through the bedroom door.
They landed with a crash in the hallway.

From the garage Max had heard and felt the
crash. He opened the glove box of the car
pulling a stainless Smith and Wesson .357
Magnum out. Spinning the cylinder he checked
to make sure it was loaded. He then headed up
the stairs meeting James half way up. When
they reached the main floor Max looked up the

stairs leading to the second floor. On the
balcony Susan and Betsey tumbled and rolled
their hands locked tightly around each
others throat. Max took the first step up the
stairs when the explosion hit.

Everything happened in slow motion. The
explosion shattered the mansions' solid oak
front door. The concussion ripped the foyer
walls apart taking ten feet of wall on both
sides. Max flew over the stairs' heavy bannister and down the twelve hard stairs that
led to the cellar. James was blown back
through the swinging door that lead to the
kitchen landing on top of the kitchen table
unconscious.

Through the massive hole that now existed
in the front of the Mansion the three men in
black raced in, their guns poised ready to
fire.

Susan felt the heavy blows of Betsey's fist
strike her face. She registered the impact but
couldn't actually feel pain only the jarring
of her circuit boards. With enough impact
Betsey could disrupt her circuits. She struck
out at Betsey hitting her in the shoulder
forcing Betsey back off her. Susan got
quickly to her feet her fists clenched. Betsey
had already rebounded from the blow and had
launched herself at Susan. Susan swung her
fist hitting Betsey square across the jaw, the
impact damaging Betsey's human outer shell.

Betsey's blood sprayed into the air as her
body sailed back through the wall to land in
another spare bedroom. Susan moved forward
only to be knocked off her feet crashing
against the dresser crushing it. She pushed
the dressers debris off her and climbed to her

feet. Betsey was on her before she could get
up. She grabbed Susan by her clothing and
lifted her off her feet hurling her through
the window that faced the front of the house.
   Susan felt herself fall then the sudden
impact of her body against the Lincoln that
sat in the driveway. The roof and windshield
shattered in embedding her between the metal.
   The three men moved swiftly up the stairs
and down the hall checking each room, their
movements reflecting their training. They
reached the room that had been Betsey's. Two
men entered and made a quick sweep. The third
remained in the hall.
   Betsey appeared out of the next room down
seeing the man standing in the hallway. She
moved swiftly and silently towards him. The
man never saw her coming, she struck him
across the jaw knocking him to the floor.
Betsey grabbed the rifle from the man and
fired point blank at the man only inches from
his body.
   His scream was deafening and it ended
quickly. She carried the gun and headed down
the stairs to the front door. Her mission had
ended and her own survival depended on getting
away so her master could recall her back. She
had gone against her own programing when she
attacked Susan and knew that she would be
punished for it. But it couldn't be helped,
she would have the last word though and her
victory would be complete.
   When she reached the bottom of the stairs
she met Martha helping Max up the cellar
stairs. She lashed out with the butt of the
rifle striking Martha across the face knocking
her out. Max fell to his knee at the top of

the stairs unable to stand on his own.

Betsey swung her foot out kicking Max in
the ribs. Max fell onto his side groaning.
Betsey kicked him onto his back and placed her
foot against his throat cutting off his supply
of air. She then lowered the rifle, the end
of the barrel pressed firmly against his head.

"Prepare to die Max Storm!" Betsey growled.

Suddenly a flash of light shot from the top
of the balcony striking Betsey's trigger hand
burning a hole clean through to the palm.
She pulled the gun up and fired the pulse of
light striking the floor of the balcony
shattering the wooden supports. The balcony
collapsed the two men it was supporting
falling with it. With a crash they became
buried under the piles of timbers and
sheetrock.

Betsey turned and headed out the gaping
hole that use to be the entrance to the
mansion. She saw Susan, her body motionless
in between the twisted metal roof of the
Lincoln. She quickly headed out into the
fields surrounding the house. She pressed her
neck just below the jaw and her eye's glowed
for an instant and then were normal again.

Max staggered to his feet his throat sore
and his legs weak. He reached down and
checked to see that Martha was still alive.
Then headed out the gaping hole after Betsey
his pistol in hand. She was quite far in
front of him when Max drew the pistol up.

"Betsey stop or I'll shoot!" Max screamed.

Betsey never turned around. Max fired, the
bullet striking her behind the knee shattering
her leg and twisting the leg outward. She
fell to the ground loosing grip on the rifle.

It banged to the ground harmlessly in front of
her. She immediately began crawling for it
but Max had reached her kicking it farther
away from her grasp. She rolled over looking
up at Max.

"You wouldn't shoot a defenseless woman
would you?" She smiled back.

"Stay where you are or I'll blow your head
off!" He snarled at her.

Betsey staggered up onto her one good knee,
the other hanging by a shred of bone and steel
rods. Her blood covered the ground and poured
from the open wound of her leg. Her arm
reached out.

"Please Max you have it all wrong, it's
Susan that is your enemy not me! Please help
me up, you've hurt me badly," Her voice
sounded sympathetic and convincing.

Max hesitated for a moment, Betsey lunged
at him knocking him down to the ground. She
clawed and scratched her way on top of him
trying to reach his pistol. Her hand locked
around his wrist bending it so the pistol
faced his head. She was breaking his wrist
and he was loosing grip on the gun. He needed
to get her off him somehow. He took his free
hand and struck her head. Succeeding only
in hurting himself.

He looked into Betsey's face, the kindness
and gentleness that was once there quickly
became replaced with terror and hatred. He
brought his good hand up digging his fingers
into her eye's. The blood spurted out into his
face and he kept digging.

Betsey shook her head trying to dislodge
his hand. She let go of his wrist to pull the

hand from her face.

Max brought the gun to bare and fired. The shell impacted against her left shoulder sending blood and metal parts out of her back. Her body tumbled off balance landing in the blood covered grass behind her. She looked back at Max rising again, her eye's gone and only brilliant green orbs showed from the dark hollows of her eyes sockets.

"Why Max? You would have been my mate. The master promised you for me."

Max fired again hitting the same shoulder and almost ripping the arm off. Betsey fell back again. Her arm hung limp and she raised her only good hand to her neck and pressed.

Instantly a bright green dot appeared and grew, rapidly enveloping her. The smaller lights began revolving around her. The force of the lights holding Max against the ground. Seconds later she disappeared. Max laid back looking at the sky, It had finally begun.

CHAPTER THIRTEEN

Calm Before the Storm

Susan struggled to get free of the automobile. Her arms pinned to her sides, she had watched helplessly Max's battle with Betsey. The metal had only given slightly against her struggling.

"Stuck?" Max asked walking up next to the car.

"Very funny, this is embarrassing."

The metal began to bend farther inch by inch, until Susan was able to wiggle herself free.

"I felt something about Betsey was wrong. Is everyone all right?" Susan said helping Max as they walked to the mansion.

"I don't know where James is. Martha is unconscious, and you were right those three men we saw in the basement were human. One stopped Betsey from blowing my head off. The last I saw, two of them became buried underneath the balcony that collapsed when Betsey shot it."

They entered the house to find James helping Martha up off the floor. There was no

sign of the men. The debris from the balcony
lay undisturbed. Susan moved forward and
began lifting most of the fallen timbers,
digging her way to the buried men. When she
found them they were both conscious.
    "Well its about time somebody got to us!"
The man coughed and looked up at Susan.
    "Are either of you injured?" She asked.
    "No, our body armor protected us. But our
companion upstairs wasn't so lucky. He's
covering the upstairs hallway."
    Max sat himself down against what was left
of the foyer wall. He looked around and
rolled his eyes.
    "The place is in shambles," Max breathed
softly.
    "It can be fixed," James said sitting on
the floor next to him.
    Martha walked up to them her face red from
the blow she received. Her eye's looked
nervously at Max then James.
    "Do . . . do you two feel like a cup of
tea?" She asked.
    James could see that she wasn't taking the
strain of what was happening around them very
well. He rose to his feet and put his arm
around her. She began to sob uncontrollably
in his arms.
    "It's all right now, let's go to the
kitchen and make that tea," James said leading
her.
    Max felt angry, this was getting out of
hand. It was beginning to affect what little
family he had left. He needed to take the
battle to them. Right now he was on the
defensive getting nowhere. Max watched the
two men climb to their feet brushing off the

dirt and fragments of wood that still clung to them. He was unaware of the small squeak that came from the open doorway.

"Holy shit man, you have one hell of a decorator!"

Max jumped with a start as he turned to see Tinker and his bodyguard Bill in the gutted out doorway. Tinker rolled himself up to Max.

"What happened LT.," Tinker looked at Max's dirty and bruised face.

"We've been double crossed, one of my group here turned out to be an Annihilator," Max shook his head as if he couldn't believe it.

"Bummer where did he go? You get him?" Tinker asked.

"Where did she go, is the question. She disappeared into the future. She also knows that we'll be coming. She doesn't know exactly when but I'm sure that the Represser will have a welcoming committee. What are you doing here so early anyway?"

"I got the stuff rather quickly, it's out in the van. I also brought a few grenade launchers, a state of the art .50 caliber with exploding rounds for Bill here and for what it's worth a good knife for everyone."

"You can keep mine, I found one hell of a sword I'll be using," Max smiled at Tinker.

"A sword? What you turnin inta Zorro or somethin?" Tinker said laughing.

"No, not really there's just something special about it, I like it, I'm attracted to it. I know it sounds strange but considering everything else that's happened."

Susan and the two men walked over to Max. The one man extended his hand.

The Time Dominators

"My name is Mead and my companion's called
Povlov. I am sorry for the devastation to
your dwelling but it couldn't be helped."

"Just who or what are you exactly and where
do you come from? And most importantly why
are you here?" Max said rising to his feet.

"Is there somewhere that we can all talk?"
Mead looked at Max then Tinker.

Max led them into the den library that
remained pretty much unscathed. Only one
wall showed the charred burns and holes from
the explosion. He motioned for everyone to
take a seat. Max eased himself down into his
favorite high back Victorian chair and looked
at Mead.

"Ok, the balls in your court," Max said.

Mead looked around the room nervously then
began.

"Well for starters we already know who each
of you are. We are from the E.U.O. which
stands for Earth Unit One. You see we're from
the future. Our mission was to destroy the
Annihilator you called Betsey before she had a
chance to kill you Max Storm. Our
intervention saved your life."

"Wait a second, I've been in the twentyfifth century. There are no humans left in
existence according to the Represser," Max cut
in.

"We are from the twentyfourth century. I
feel it's best that you know the whole story.
Please bare with me, Earth had become a
utopia. All diseases were wiped out and the
human life span extended to 125 years. We
totally cleaned the environment and life
flourished.

We had even made contact with other planets

in our solar system. The need to know was
great, our desire for the unknown even
greater. We needed to be the first to venture
outside our system. But with all our
technology we hadn't developed a way to
sustain life for longer periods. So we turned
to cybernetics. We felt that we could create
a machine that could survive, to explore deep
space.

That's when we came up with the CS1."

"The CS . . . what?" Tinker broke in.

"The CS1, it stands for Cybernetic Space 1.
It was the ultimate in cybernetic technology
designed to withstand the ultimate harshness
of space.

But something went wrong. They had
programed its function, but on July 24th
3073 it became self aware. It escaped killing
twelve people. A massive search ensued only
resulting in more deaths. Then slowly as each
day passed we began finding more and more
Cybernetic robots destroying and eliminating
huge populations of people.

The Annihilators as you call them, became
an epidemic like the
A.I.D.S disease that will soon emerge in your
culture. But unlike your disease we couldn't
destroy them quick enough. They began to over
run us all over the world.

We called out to our distant stellar
neighbors for help, none of them responded
except for the Stolic's."

"Who or what was the Stolic's?" Susan spoke
as she moved in back of Max's chair.

Just then James and Martha appeared
carrying two large trays, one containing a big
silver tea pot with cups and saucers and the

usual complements. The other was full of
sandwiches.

"Please everybody, grab something to eat,
you all need to keep your strength up,"
Martha said placing the tray down on one of
the coffee tables.
James did the same and began flipping the
cups over filling them with tea. Everyone
moved forward to grab a cup and a sandwich.
Mead and Povlov grabbed two or three each.
Max notice this and wondered what the human
race had been reduced to.

"Have I missed anything?" James asked.

"Not really James, these Jo's are from the
twentythird century. They were just lettin
us in on the Represser's birth and rise to
power," Tinker spoke with a full mouth.

Mead turned to Susan and smiled.

"The Stolic's are a race of very emotional
people. Their emotions guide everything in
their lives. They look fairly similar to us
only they're completely hairless. Their
planet is towards the Andromeda galaxy. They
responded to our plea for help but sent only
two hundred soldiers. We were surprised when
they didn't send more aid. But we soon
learned why.

They were armed only with swords. The
easiest way for me to describe them is . . . ,"

"A Japanese Ninja sword, with a diamond
handle with rubies and emeralds buried into
the diamond. The scabbard looks like gold but
is virtually weightless," Max cut in.

Mead looked at him with a little surprise
on his face.

"How do you know this?" Mead asked.

"I have one in the cellar, I used it to get

away from the Represser before," Max took a
sip of his tea.

"You should feel honored! The sword when
made, bonds with only one
Stolic. They have that sword until they die,
then the sword is destroyed with them. The
sword has an essence of its own, it doesn't
think but it reacts with the Stolic's emotions
using them as energy to feed power to itself.
It's fabled to have many different uses not
just as a weapon. It was the life line of the
Stolic's.

There has never been a human who has been
able to make the sword function. There was a
legend that a man would come, a great man who
would bind with the sword and help reclaim
this planet."

Max didn't look surprised, he understood
now what had happened. The sword had bonded
with him. It fed off his hatred from the
death of his mother giving him the power to
destroy the attacking Annihilators.

"The Stolic's battled fiercely along side
us, we nearly succeeded in destroying the
Represser. Then the tables turned and slowly
each of the Stolic's were annihilated along
with a few million more of the human race. We
called them requesting more men but they
responded with a plan instead. We would
immigrate to their planet until we could
destroy the Represser and reclaim the planet.

We planned our escape, and we only managed
to get a little over a million people to the
Stolic's planet. The Annihilators found out
and destroyed many of our ships before they
could take off," Mead stopped talking as if
trying to remember what happened next.

The Time Dominators

"What's left of the human race exists on the planet Comm. We have been making attacks on the Represser for about seventy years now. Each has met in failure, every one there after was deemed a suicide mission. But we still come, our planet is important to us, we are it's last hope. Then we discovered that your father Sam Storm had discovered the secret of time travel. The time travel information was the one thing the Represser didn't have.

Thousands gave their lives to keep it from him. Then your father came into the picture giving the secret for a measly power unit and a grafted human computer. No disrespect Susan . . . ," Mead looked her way.

"None taken," Susan looked irritated.

Max felt her hands slowly touch his shoulders. Her touch was soft and gentle but became tense when Mead commented on her existence. Max also could see the anger in Meads face. Sam Storm had unknowingly sold out the human race.

"Now as a result of that mistake, The Annihilators have set up bases throughout time. They will soon begin to conquer the very existence of the human race," Mead waved his arms in the air.

"Can time be altered? Can major events be changed?" Max questioned him.

"You mean to tell me you've been using that time machine of your fathers and you don't know how it effects time?" Mead looked irritated and surprised.

Max shook his head no.

"Time as we know it cannot be changed. Everything that happens is supposed to happen. The only way to change it is by causing someone from that time period to change it for you. For instance, if an Annihilator went back and absorbed Adolf Hitler, then time could be altered from that point on."

"But I thought that the person needed to be from that era," Susan said.

"They do, but you changed all that Susan. You were the first cell to chip link. After they found out it worked they began capturing humans and turning them into inhuman atrocities. They now could pass totally as a human and interact and eventually dominate."

Susan's hands again tensed on Max's shoulders. Max understood, it hurt her to listen to Mead tell of her inhumanity. What Mead didn't understand was that despite Susan's physical make up she was still a human and constructed from human cells that guide her thought patterns and emotions.

Max would speak to Mead later about making that same mistake again.

Max looked at Mead, the man looked about forty but was most likely only twentyfive or so. There were many wrinkles across his face and many scars. His hair was dark brown and already showed signs of graying. He stood around six foot and with his body armor his form looked twice the size. Povlov was different though, he stood about five inches shorter. His hair sandy colored and his face showing more innocence than Meads. Max hadn't heard him utter a sound yet and he wondered why.

"Povlov, what do you feel of the situation were in?" Max thought of something to try and get him to speak.

Povlov upon hearing his name looked at

The Time Dominators

Max.

"He's Russian, but he understands English. He couldn't speak even if he wanted to. We were intercepted on our way here by two Annihilators. In the course of our battle Povlov's throat became injured rendering him speechless. Because of our state of the art medicinal practices we were able to repair the damage quickly but the technology for repair of the vocal cords could only be done back on Comm," Povlov smiled saying nothing.

"What plans do we have now?" James asked.

"I think we should go ahead with our original plan to assault the Represser and hopefully destroy him," Mead replied.

"It won't be as easy as it sounds," Max spoke up reaching for another sandwich.

"I think we should try and knock out their main power supply. I appeared in a conduit room next to the main reactor. If we could knock it out then we might have a chance on reaching the Represser," Susan spoke up.

"How big is their power supply?" Mead quickly shot back.

"It feeds the entire planet, if we can generate a big enough explosion then it might cause a chain reaction destroying their existence all at once," Susan answered.

"It might just work! We have been trying to get to the Represser assuming everything was controlled through him. If there is just one power supply then we might have a chance!"

"Don't worry about generatin a big enough kaboom, leave that to ole Tinker," Tinker said thumbing his chest.

"Well then it looks like we have a plan.

We have this evening to square away the details and get a good nights rest," Max commanded taking charge.

"I'll have a good meal planned for dinner tonight, all of you should go get cleaned up. You look like you were all playing in dirt!" Martha said trying to get everyone to laugh.

As if by her command everyone began filing out of the den.

"Follow me Mead, I'll show you were you and Povlov will be staying tonight," Max motioned for him to follow.

When they reached the top of the stairs Max cringed in disgust. The body of Meads third soldier lay twisted and broken in the middle of the hall. The walls on both sides of him splattered with blood.

"He was young Max, inexperienced, I never should have allowed him to come," Mead spoke softly.

Max turned and looked at him nodding. There were many times in Nam that he had come across the same thing. Green kids who had no right being there. Yes, Max sympathized with what Mead was feeling. Mead stepped forward and folded the large rug that laid beneath him around his fallen companion. He then reached to the side of the belt he wore and pressed a button. A little red light lit up on his belt. Moments later a green light appeared in the middle of the fallen man. Max knew they were transporting him back through time. It ended quickly leaving only the blood splat-tered walls to show that a man had been slain there.

"The others aboard our ship will dispose of the body. He will be buried in space like all

the others. None of us will be buried on
Earth until we have succeeded in our mission,"
Mead spoke solemnly.

Max said nothing, he continued on down the
hallway leading to the third undamaged spare
bedroom.

"Showers in the back, clean towels are
already in there," Max motioned for them to
stay put.

He went into the master bedroom and
returned carrying two bathrobes.

"Here's something to put on after you take
a shower, they should fit you fine. Povlov
will be swimming a little in it," Max
smiled.

Mead and Povlov accepted the garments looking
at each other baffled. They shrugged and
walked into the bedroom. Susan walked up next
to Max.

"Now that you gave them my bedroom where do
you expect me to sleep?" She asked. Max
laughed and walked down the hall to the master
bedroom. He turned and motioned with his
finger for her to follow. Susan followed and
closed the door behind her.

Tinker and his bodyguard had followed James
and Martha into the kitchen. Martha began to
make dinner. James came up behind her patting
her on the shoulder.

"I'll give Tinker and Bill my room, if you
don't mind me staying with you tonight," James
winked at her.

Martha smiled and nodded. They had known
each other for most of their lives. They had
a relationship off and on through the years
but neither wanted to commit totally to the
other. At their age now the understanding

they had between one another was perfect.
They loved the companionship and the few
occasional nights they spent together.

James told Tinker and Bill to follow him.
Martha continued to prepare dinner.

Mead had taken his shower and finally
figured out how the bathrobe was worn. He
motioned for Pavlov to use the bathroom.
Pavlov disappeared closing the door.

Mead looked out the large bay window at the
green mountains. It was such a contrast to
earth in the twentyfifth century. He
remembered hearing the elders talk about how
Earth had been. Of how it looked green and
alive just as it did here. The more he looked
the more transfixed he became. He felt he had
a divine purpose, the Represser had stripped
the planet of all life, at least life as he
knew it.

All the trees were gone everything that was
beautiful had vanished. Replaced by cities
full of Annihilators and metal monsters.
Where the cites ended were huge deserts. Some
of the men that tried to attack the Represser
before managed to escape into the deserts.
They never were heard from again, and when
recalled their time belts would malfunction.

Some theorized on what was out there saying
there were huge genetic mutations that
savagely tore the men to pieces. Others say
the extreme heat had killed them and rendered
their transportation devices useless. Mead
didn't know what to believe, he only knew that
the time may come when he would be forced into
the vast wasteland.

Susan had walked up to Max wrapping her
arms around his neck. She gently closed her

eyes and pressed her lips against his feeling
the influx of signals from his touch. Max
returned her kiss holding her close. Then he
pulled away looking into her eye's. Susan
grabbed him by the hand and headed towards the
bathroom.

"What are you doing?" Max stopped and
asked.

"We're going to take a shower together,"
She looked back and tugged on his hand.

"Why don't you take your shower first then
I'll take mine," Max suggested.

"Don't you want me?" Susan sounded hurt.

"Yes . . . I do but not right now. I don't
think it's right for either of us now," Max
tried to explain.

He wanted nothing more than to follow her
into the bathroom and make love to her. He
felt something for her he had never felt for
anyone before. He also felt he was treading
on loose ground. If a relationship between
Susan and himself ever happened it would occur
on its own and not from some half hour fling.
He respected her and felt she should
be treated like a lady. He also understood
that she had been given her freedom to
physically touch and feel again. And that
meant she wanted the sensation not so much the
relationship that might go with it.

"No," He thought "When the time is right
we'll both know it."

Max stepped forward and grabbed Susan by
the shoulders and kissed her hard on the lips.
Susan closed her eyes and sighed. She understood that now wasn't the time and that Max
would eventually be the one for her. She
didn't know how long it would take but knew it

would eventually happen.   He had given
her time to think about what she was doing.

She was so starved for the physical touch
of a human that she overlooked that it might
jeopardize a special relationship that first
had to start with friendship.

She turned and headed into the bathroom
closing the door.   Part of her felt sad but
another part felt she had done right.

Max grabbed his change of clothes and
headed down to the spare bedroom that Betsey
had used.   He'd take his shower there away
from the temptation.   It had taken every ounce
of will not to climb in with her, and he knew
that if he stayed his will would have broken
easily.

Max had finished his shower and had donned
a pair of sweat pants and a tank top.   He
headed down the small set of spiral stairs
that led to the kitchen.   There he saw Martha
pulling a large roast out of the oven.   On top
were various pots filled with mash potatoes
and vegetables.   She turned and saw Max
standing there.

"Maxwell could you get a set of pot holders
and take this into the dining room?   The
others are already in there except for Susan."

Max grabbed a set of pot holders and picked
up the large roasting pot.   He backed through
the two swinging doors that from the kitchen
to the dinning room.

"Hey LT., I'll grab ya a beer," Tinker
spoke up.

"Can you pour me a glass of wine instead?"
Max asked setting the pan down.

"Sure thing LT., you want to drink that
French stuff tonight it's OK with me.   Just

remember the headaches it gives you the next
mornin! Like that time in Bangkok when we
both had a three day pass?" Tinker winked at
Max.

Martha came through the doors carrying
another two pots.

Mead and Povlov were dressed in the
bathrobes that Max had given them. They sat
at the table, Mead saying nothing. Max sat
down at the head, Tinker and Bill to the
left and two chairs down. Mead and Povlov
sat to Max's right.

"Has anyone seen Susan?" Max asked. As soon
as he said it, she walked through the swinging
doors carrying two more pots.

Max rose from his chair, Susan was dressed
in Max's purple silk royal bathrobe. Her hair
was blown dry and flowed in perfect form to
her attire. She had on a set of earrings that
Max recognized to be his mothers. Mead turned
to see Susan and his mouth dropped open, he
rose from his chair.

"I hope I'm not late," Susan smiled.

"Not at all dear, please be seated," Martha
pointed to the chair by Max.

Susan walked around the table, Max looked
at her legs that were perfectly shaped and he
noticed she had bare feet. He helped her with
the chair and returned to his own.

The meal went on without anybody talking
about the mission tomorrow. Everyone seemed
festive and happy. They all complimented
Martha on her cooking expertise. All thoughts
of the nightmares and horrors both past and
present vanished at least for the night.

Mead and Povlov both seemed to have
problems eating. They studied their food with

particular interest until Max found out that in their time food like Max understood it, was nonexistent. Mead then began taking particular attention to Susan. Max noticed it but didn't pay any attention, Susan was on her own and old enough to do the things she liked.

"Susan, I don't understand why you bother eating. You don't need food to survive," Mead commented.

"I eat because I choose to. My sensors can determine a particular foods flavor and consistency. I cannot taste like you can but can still enjoy food like you do," Susan explained.

Max rose from the table carrying his plate and a few of the empty pots to the kitchen. James rose and did the same.

"What are your plans now?" James asked.

"Well, I was going to ask everyone if they wished to retire to the den for an after dinner drink. I was going to start the fireplace," Max said.

"That is a good idea, huh, Martha and I won't be attending. Please wake me when you rise," James smiled and began helping Martha.

Max never understood why they never married. They had virtually been his parents over the years. Neither dated, and when there was an activity they both went together. He had asked James why he never married and he had always said," I'll marry when you do." Max smiled, he knew James knew him like a book. Max headed back into the dinning room.

"I'll be serving nightcaps in the den if everyone would like to join me."

"I'll come," Susan said raising her hand.

"Count me in," Tinker followed.

"I'll pass," Tinkers bodyguard Bill said.

"I'll pass also," Mead said, Povlov also shook his head.

"Povlov and myself will be taking turns tonight keeping guard. We don't need any surprises this evening," Mead said.

Max shrugged and pushed his chair in heading for the den. Susan and Tinker followed. Mead turned and headed upstairs to get some sleep, Povlov taking the first watch. Max left the door to the den open in case Povlov wished to join them.

Susan snickered seeing Povlov standing in the shattered foyer cradling his rifle in his arms.

"He looks hilarious standing there in that bathrobe holding the rifle," Susan laughed covering her mouth.

Tinker also broke out laughing. Max finally joined in. He then filled a small snifter with Drambuie and walked it out to Povlov.

"Here, this will help you stay awake," Max smiled handing it to him.

Povlov smiled and accepted the drink. Max motioned for him to come in the den and join them. Povlov looked up the stairs then at his watch. He then nodded and followed Max into the den.

Max and Tinker started reciting hilarious times they had together causing everyone, even Povlov to smile and laugh. Susan became enthralled listening to Max tell stories about the mischief he'd gotten into. Hours had quickly passed and Tinker slowly began to drop off. Povlov looked at his watch and tapped Max on the arm pointing upstairs. Povlov had to go and wake Mead for his watch. Max nodded.

Max picked up Tinker and layed him onto the sofa in the back of the den. Tinker did what he always liked to do, bury himself in a bottle. Max always thought Tinker did it to get rid of the demons that haunted him from the Vietnam war.

"I'll be upstairs, come up when ever you wish," Max said to Susan.

"Will you be waiting for me?" Susan smiled back.

Max left shaking his head. He climbed the kitchen stairs meeting Mead halfway up.

"Sleep well?" Max asked.

"I haven't slept on a real bed in years! I slept better in the last few hours then I could ever remember. By the way Max Storm, tomorrow could bring success or death. I just want you to know that your kindness to us and your help is appreciated immensely."

Max patted him on the shoulder and continued up the stairs. It was a nice thing for Mead to thank him, but to even surmise that they could die tomorrow Max had always looked at the statement as a jinx. He didn't listen to it in Nam and he wouldn't listen to it here.

When he reached the bedroom he grabbed a spare blanket out of the closet and folded it out over a small chair forming a single bed, he'd give Susan the bed. It didn't take long for him to drop off into a deep sleep.

Susan sat on the floor staring at the fire. She held out her hand near the flames. She could sense the heat but couldn't feel it. She watched the flames dance around the wood as it burned. There was so much she needed to catch up on. So many sensations and things to experience all over again.

Mead took up his position in the foyer standing as Povlov had done earlier. He heard the crackle of the fire and walked over to the den's entrance. He peeked in seeing Susan sitting on the floor staring at the fire. Walking in he came up next to Susan.

"Very peaceful is it not?" He said softly.

"Yes it is, there's much I have missed out on," Susan began.

"Having a body again is all I ever wanted. Now I find myself looking to do all the things I couldn't do before."

"Well that's understandable," Mead said softly bringing his face close to her ear.

He reached out and touched her hair running his fingers through it. Susan closed her eye's accepting the sensations input. Mead then began kissing her ears and neck. Susan sighed letting him continue. The stimuli was too great and she longed for the impute of raw emotion. Her human cells cried out for more. Mead stopped and looked into her eye's.

"Let's get out of this room there's some form of water tub in the next room," Mead grabbed her hand leading her into the garden space where the whirlpool tub was. He flipped the cover off letting the steam rise from the warm water. He propped the rifle against the wall and took off his bathrobe and slid into the hot water.

Susan untied her bathrobe letting it fall to the floor. She stood there for a moment seeing the satisfaction in Mead's face. She then slid in the hot water next to him. He put his arm around her and drew his lips down to hers. Soon their passion grew, Susan taking in every sensation and feeling. It was very intense for her and something she hadn't experienced for years. Mead was enjoying it just as much, she could tell by his expressions. Then it ended leaving Mead slouched down in the tub a triumphant smile across his face.

Susan didn't want it to end but knew it must be. She curled up next to him and ran her fingers down the middle of his chest.

"Are you born at birth to go on these missions?" She asked.

"No, we develop much like any other humans. Although we lack many of the things that even this time period provides. We grow, go to school, marry have kids, just like everyone else. But men and women are chosen at random. We can refuse to go but it is a great disgrace."

"So you were picked early then," Susan asked evading the real question.

"What do you mean early? They chose me just as my second child was born! I have not seen my wife or kids in five years!" Mead said dropping the bombshell.

Susan pulled away from him hurt immensely by his words. She had done it again, just like before. She climbed quickly out of the tub and slipped her bathrobe on and headed out the door. She felt disgusted, she had made the same mistake twice. She had made love to a married man.

Mead sat in the tub and leaned back, he felt no wrong for his actions. He hadn't been with a woman since he left his wife. He didn't break his vows to her either, Susan wasn't human she was only a machine, a machine made to serve.

Susan climbed the kitchen stairs and raced down the hall to the master bedroom. She went into the bathroom and cleaned herself up. Splashing water on her face she looked into the mirror. She felt horrible, used and dirty. She stepped from the bathroom into the dark bedroom.

Her vision instantly switched to infra-red allowing her to see clearly. At the far end of the room was Max sound asleep. He had been a gentleman leaving her the bed. She slipped the bathrobe off and climbed between the sheets staring at the ceiling. Feeling uneasy she got up grabbing her blanket and walked over to where Max was sleeping. She flopped down on the floor next to him wrapping the blanket around her.

She noticed the plug that protruded from the wall. She accessed her memory on recharging. Pulling the blanket off her leg she exposed the leg band. On the inside of the band, she pulled at one of the dark open ports pulling a round tube connected to a cord. The tube folded open revealing four corners. She leaned over to the wall plug and placed the opened tube in front of it. The tube instantly locked onto the plug with the four magnetized ends. The flow of electrical energy connected instantly to her internal power supply unit. She leaned over and rested her head on the edge of the chair and turned herself off.

CHAPTER FOURTEEN

Into Tomorrow

Max treaded through the hallway as silently as possible. His only means of escape was to be as stealthy as he could. He wondered though where he'd escape to, there was desert all around him, his survival looked bleak. He was the last person in the assault party left. The others were eliminated, only he had managed to escape. There came a bright light at the end of the hallway. It seemed to draw him forward, he couldn't take his eye's off it. When he reached it the hallway opened up into a large circular room. Lights mounted in the walls shined on the catwalk that went along the inner rim of the room.

Max looked down, there was only darkness and the sound of water running. Looking up, there was a little dot of light where the surface was. He guessed he had to be a mile or so down. He stepped into the room moving along the catwalk. His sword poised ready for an attack. He was tired, dirty and beyond all else thirsty. The water below seemed to

attract him and he looked down every so often.
All along the walls were tunnel entrances.
One of them had to lead outside, but
which one?

Then came the clang of metal against metal.
Max turned to see the Represser enter the
room, throngs of Annihilators following him.

"You thought you could escape me Max
Storm!" The Represser yelled at Max.

The Annihilators advanced getting closer
and closer. Max lunged out with the sword
it's energy crackling off the blade. Two
Annihilators instantly dropped falling off the
catwalk into the dark oblivion below. Beams
of light shot out striking the wall next to
him gouging out big chunks of concrete. Max
fought his way towards the Represser. The
Annihilators dropped one by one. Max saw a
break in the fight and climbed up on the
catwalks railing. He launched himself over
the dark void below, sword in hand towards the
Represser. He landed against the railing in
front of him.

The Represser reached out to force him into
the darkness below. Max flailed the sword back
and forth keeping the Represser away while he
managed to get over the railing onto the
catwalk. Max drove the sword through the
Represser's chest but he kept advancing until
they locked arms. The Represser's strength
was unbelievable. He picked Max up like a rag
doll and tossed him over the railing. Max
managed to grab hold of the sword causing the
Represser to loose balance and tumble off the
catwalk with him. They fell, the darkness
enveloping them. Then they both made contact
with the water Max had heard. The Represser

was still functioning and Max felt his hands
lock around his throat. The Represser forced
Max beneath the water to drown him. All Max
could see was the hideous glow of the
Represser's green eyes.

Max awoke coughing and gagging. The sweat
poured off his body in beads. The room was
dark and still and for a moment he thought he
had died. Then he began to remember where he
was.

"Max are you all right?" Susan asked
activating herself.

"Huh, yeh I guess so. I just had a
nightmare," Max said dazed.

"Was it worse than normal?" Susan asked.

She remembered all the years before when
she had scanned the house regularly and the
nightmares Max grew up having were a nightly
occurrence.

"Yes this was a bad one," Max said trying
to remember exactly what it was about but
found he couldn't.

Susan pulled herself up onto the edge of
Max's bed. The blanket had fallen off but she
didn't care. Max couldn't see her in the
dark.

"Are you sure you're all right?" Susan
asked again.

"Yes, Susan I'm fine now. What time is
it?" He asked diverting the question.

"Its 4:55am," Susan said.

"We probably should be getting up. We'll
be leaving in an hour or so."

Max raised himself on his elbows. Susan
pushed him back down laying her head on his
chest. Max could feel her nakedness against
his own.

The Time Dominators

"To what honor do I deserve this?" He said
softly to her.

"Nothing, I'm just glad that you're my
friend. You show me respect even though you
know I'm not totally human."

"But to me you are human," Max said
softly.

Susan looked up at him, she could see his
face but he couldn't see hers. She drew her
lips up to his and kissed him running her
fingers through his hair. Then she grabbed
the blanket and wrapped herself up in it. She
walked over to the nightstand beside the bed
and turned on the light. Max turned and
looked at her standing by the nightstand with
just the blanket wrapped around her.

Susan walked back over and sat on the edge
of Max's bed. She wanted to tell Max what had
happened between her and Mead but found the
words wouldn't form in her voice activator.
Max saw the concern in her face.

"Hey is something wrong? You can tell me,
I'll listen," Max said. He reached out and
rubbed his hand over her shoulder.

Susan closed her eye's feeling his touch.
It was different than Meads, it was electric.
She opened her eye's and looked at Max wishing
she could cry.

"Hold me Max, just hold me."

She fell into his arms, Max held her tight
not knowing what to make of the situation.
All he knew was that something was bothering
her.

James awoke alone in the bed. He watched
the ceiling fan slowly rotate and wondered
what the day would bring, victory or defeat.
He hauled himself out of bed and into the

shower. He heard a clank on the shower door.
Opening it slowly he was greeted by Martha
standing there with a hot cup of tea.

"Hurry up with your shower, I have
breakfast almost on the table," She
smiled reaching in and smacking him on the
behind.

James almost spilled his tea giving her an
irritated look. Martha went back to the
kitchen where Tinker and Bill sat drinking
coffee.

"You get the old buzzard up?" Tinker
asked.

"He's already in the shower," Martha said
returning to the stove.

"If ya don't mind my opinion, why haven't
you two married yet?" Tinker asked her.

"Cause my young friend we like things just
the way they are," She said not stopping what
she was doing.

Tinker shrugged his shoulders at Bill who
smiled back. Povlov came in wearing his
battle armor. Mead came in shortly after that
dressed the same way.

"Is Max up yet?" Mead asked.

"I ain't seen him," Tinker said looking
back.

Povlov reached down and felt Tinkers stumps
where his legs had been.

"No they ain't curled up underneath me or
nothin. Their actually gone," Tinker looked
irritated. Povlov disappeared from the room.

"Where's he goin?" Tinker asked Mead.

"Don't know, wait and find out," Mead said
giving him no clue.

He knew that Povlov had headed to the
basement where the time machine was. He also

knew that he was going to construct a pair of
simple mechanical legs for Tinker. With
various parts from computers and other
electronics it would be a simple task. It was
done on Comm a lot when people loose limbs,
only theirs were much more advanced and
lifelike. But Tinker would at least be
able to walk again.

Max stepped into the shower, he knew Martha
probably had breakfast on the table already
but he wasn't hungry. He never ate before a
battle his stomach couldn't take it. He
propped himself up against the wall underneath
the stream of water. The water was extremely
hot yet Max felt chills as it cascaded down
his body. Was his dreams about drowning real?
He wondered if they had any meaning. It was
strange to him that the dream was always the
same, until this one. This nightmare was
different though, it felt real! Max grabbed
the bar of soap and began washing trying to
take his mind off the dream.

Susan watched Max go into the bathroom.
She let the blanket fall to the floor and
walked over to pick up her clothes. She
walked past the large stand up mirror and
hesitated looking at herself. She turned and
spun herself in the mirror. She was every bit
human looking as anyone else would be. The
only thing that differentiated her from a
human was the stainless steel leg band. It
was a distinct reminder that she would never
be totally human. She also couldn't cry, she
hadn't been built for it. Her vision
automatically went to infra-red in the dark.
She would never experience the darkness of
night or a dark room.

The more she began to think about the difference the more she began to feel less human.

Susan was preoccupied and hadn't heard the door open behind her. Mead stepped in staring at her naked form in front of the mirror. Susan saw the reflection and spun around covering her nakedness with her clothes.

"What are you doing here?" She snapped.

"I came to check on you and Max," Mead smiled looking at her. He walked up to her looking directly into her eye's.

"I could stand for another romp in that water tub," Mead said grabbing her hand. Susan didn't budge an inch.

"What are you doing? Come on, I order you! You are built to serve are you not?"

Suddenly Max walked through the bathroom door. Susan moved forward bring her free hand up slapping Mead hard across the face. The impact knocked him back onto the bed. She then turned and looked at Max feeling ashamed. She walked past him into the bathroom and shut the door.

"Damn machine! It's built to serve man, it's no wonder why the Represser took over the planet! You better deactivate her after the mission ends. If you don't, I will!" Mead said rolling over to get up.

Max walked over and extended his hand to help Mead up. Mead grabbed his hand and slowly stood up. Max brought his fist around hitting Mead hard across the jaw knocking onto the bed then over onto the floor.

"What the hell? What did you do that for?"

Mead snapped.

"From this moment on you will show Susan the same respect that you would show any human. And so help me if you lay one hand on her again I'll . . . ," Max pointed his finger sternly at Mead, then stormed out of the bedroom.

Max headed downstairs, his anger flaring. He burst into the kitchen where James, Martha, Tinker, and Bill sat eating breakfast.

"Here, sit down and eat," Martha said handing him a plate of food.

"Not now, thank you Martha. I really don't feel hungry," Max walked over and poured himself a cup of coffee.

James walked over and placed his plate into the sink. He came up behind Max.

"What's wrong Max?" James asked.

"Nothing, I just woke up on the wrong side of the bed," Max said taking a sip of his coffee.

"Frankly Max, I don't believe you. I've known you for too long not to know when it's something more important."

Max picked his coffee cup up and motioned for James to follow him. He headed out of the kitchen and into the den.

"James, I'm just disgusted with human beings as a whole. I just caught Mead upstairs forcing Susan to have sex. He said that she's just a machine like the Annihilators, built to serve humans. Even in the twentyfifth century people still have little regard or respect for life."

"You have to understand Max what happened to the human race. They were wiped off the face of the planet. Probably by machines like

Susan. Mead was brought up hating and
despising machines that resemble humans. I
think you should tell me what is really
bothering you. Did Susan agree to Mead's
advances?"

"No, she slapped him across the face," Max
looked up at James.

"Then it sounds to me that you're jealous.
Do you have feelings for Susan?" James asked.

"Well . . . she's a very beautiful woman.
I don't see her as a machine, she's so much
more. I guess I do have feelings for her,"
Max nodded his head.

"Then you should tell her how you feel. Be
honest with each other. I think you two make
an excellent pair," James smiled rising to
his feet.

He didn't want to tell Max that his father
had also felt the same way about Susan when
she was human so many years ago.

James left the room leaving Max to ponder
his feelings.

"Am I falling in love with Susan?" Max
thought to himself.

He quickly dismissed this thought. It was to
soon even beginning to think about that. He
didn't even know Susan fully. Maybe given
time their relationship would build but
right now their only link to one another was
the war against the Represser, after that,
who knows? Susan may want to leave and lead
her own life. Max stood up and headed back to
the kitchen to refill his coffee cup. He had
to clear his mind. Going into battle with
excess emotional baggage would only cause
disaster. He had a score to settle with the
Represser and nothing would stop him.

The Time Dominators

Only he didn't realize that he was being
driven by revenge and that in itself could be
the greatest emotional baggage.

Mead entered the kitchen and sat down at
the table. Martha sat a plate of food down in
front of him. Tinker looked at Mead.

"Wow man, where did you get that fat lip?"
Tinker smiled.

Mead slowly raised his eye's looking at him
not saying a word. Then he began eating.
James smiled, he sometimes liked the way
Tinker skirted around situations. Tinker
was blunt, direct and very opinionated and
James like that. Max entered the kitchen
pouring himself another cup of coffee.

"Ok, folks we need to get our gear ready.
Tinker where are the supplies you brought?"
Max asked.

"Their right inside the van outside LT,"
Tinker motioned for Bill to go out and get
them. The big man lumbered away from the
table and headed outside.

"We will probably be detected as soon as we
arrive. I'm sure Betsey has warned the
Represser that we were coming. We have to be
ready to hold back their advances to allow
Tinker and Bill enough time to place the
charges. The rest will be up to Susan. She
has to be able to get us in and out of there
as quickly as possible," Max said.

"Did I hear my name mentioned?" Susan said
as she entered the room.

"Will you be able to start the time machine
quickly in order to get us out of there?" Max
said turning towards her.

She was dressed in the one piece gold suit,
its clinginess almost took Max's breath away.

The Time Dominators

"I can activate the time sequence in seconds," Susan said smiling, noticing Max's stare along with everyone else.

"Good, then in fifteen minutes we'll meet in the basement at the time machine," Max took another long gulp of his coffee and headed out of the kitchen followed by Tinker.

Max helped Tinker and his wheelchair down the stairs to the basement.

"You know LT. for all the time I spend here you
should put a service lift in."

"I'll consider it if we make it back," Max said softly.

Tinker felt uneasy, it was the first time Max had ever sounded negative about a mission. Max wheeled him into the workshop where the machine was.

Entering the room they saw Povlov standing in the corner working on something.

"Povlov, ole buddy whatcha workin on?" Tinker said wheeling over to him.

Povlov turned around holding two mechanical legs fashioned out of spare computer parts and various pieces of metal that lay around the shop. They looked like legs but more of a conglomerated patchwork of metal. They wouldn't win any beauty contest but hopefully would allow Tinker to stand.

From the sides of the legs ran one thick wire up to a regular belt. On the back of the belt was a small box, each wire running directly into it.

Povlov reached over and grabbed Tinkers folded pant legs pulling them out. He then cut a slit up the side of each exposing the stumps of Tinkers legs. Tinker watched in

The Time Dominators

fascination as Povlov clamped each mechanical leg to what remained of his own. He wrapped the belt around Tinkers waist and pushed a small button on the side of the box.

Povlov backed away and motioned for Tinker to stand up and walk towards him. Tinker shrugged and pulled himself up allowing his weight to rest on the legs. He felt a slight throbbing where the box touched his back. Tinker removed his hands off the arm rests and stood up straight.

"My god LT.! I'm standing, I can't believe it! I just can't believe it!" Tinker yelled in joy.

Povlov still motioned for him to walk towards him. Tinkers legs moved slow at first scuffing the floor with each step. Tinker wobbled from side to side as each leg moved. He slowly became more confident and each step became easier. In a matter of minutes he was walking around the room like his legs had always been there. Mead walked into the room and watched Tinker walking around. He then walked up to Max.

"It's good to see the legs Povlov constructed work well," Mead said.

"How does it work?" Tinker asked.

"Your brain and spine provide the neural communications to various muscles in your body enabling it to move. The box that hooks on the back of the belt takes those impulses that are still there and channels them into the mechanical legs. He'll have no feeling in them but he will have movement."

"Fascinating!" Max said softly in awe of what he just witnessed.

Tinker walked over and shook Povlov's hand

The Time Dominators

and then gave him a big hug. Max could see
Tinkers eye's they were almost in tears.
Tinker gained the one thing back that he
always wanted. The others filed into the room
and stared at Tinker walking around. Bill
dropped the gear and stared, his mouth open.
Mead walked up to Tinker and placed a hand on
his shoulder.

"There is one downfall to this," Mead
said.

Tinker looked at him as if the axe was now
suddenly going to fall.

"When you become physically and more
importantly mentally fatigued the legs will
also be affected and will not function
properly. You must over time, condition
yourself always to stay mentally alert when
your using them."

"No problem," Tinker said relieved.

Max turned and began sorting through the
gear Tinker brought. He handed James a
grenade launcher with a belt of grenades. He
pulled the same out for himself. He picked up
the .50 caliber sniper rifle and felt its
heavy weight. He then handed it to Bill along
with the extra rounds.

Tinker reached down and picked up a M16
rifle with a belt full of clips.

"The rest is yours Tinker," Max said.
Bill automatically began loading the cases
into the machine. Susan walked in
looking Mead in the eye and giving him a dirty
look. Mead smiled and stepped into the
machine.

Martha had come down also, she grabbed Max
by the arm and reached up to give a kiss.

"Be careful Maxwell and remember what we

talked about," She whispered to him.
Max nodded and headed towards the machine with
Susan. Martha then stopped James as he began
to follow.

"James, please be careful, and come back in
one piece. I don't like the idea of you going
with them but if you have to, then please just
come back for me," She reached up and kissed
him on the lips.

"Don't worry, I'm just going to look after
Max. You take care until I come back," He
smiled giving her what reassurance he could.

James headed into the machine with the
others. Susan moved up to the panel and
touched the wires that hung from the open
section of the console.

"Max could you ask the others to please
turn around? I have to strip out of my
clothes to hook up these wires," Susan said
showing him the connections.

Max had everyone turn around and he nodded
to Susan to begin. Susan stripped out of her
clothes, she looked up to see Max turn his
head like the others. She smiled, he was
definitely a gentleman. Hooking up each wire
sections of the machine began to power up.
She hooked the last wire up which connected
her to the ships power supply. She needed to
do this to engage the time displacement unit.

She checked all the systems that were
operational making sure they functioned
properly. She imputed the correct time
sequence and date.

"Are we ready Max?" She asked.

"When ever you are Susan," Max said as
everyone began loading their weapons.

Susan started the time displacement unit.

She felt the influx of power into her body as
the machine powered up for time transport.
    Martha watched the small green dot appear
and grow to envelop the entire machine. The
smaller multicolored lights then began to
rotate around the machine. Moments later it
vanished.

The Time Dominators

CHAPTER FIFTEEN

WAR!

Susan was monitoring the ships transport
when she detected the sudden malfunction.
There was an abnormal surge of power from the
ships' storage cell. She tried to compensate
for the increase in energy but found that the
more she adjusted the more came. She couldn't
control it.

"Max! There is a . . . malfunction in the
. . . power storage cell. I can not . . .
compensate for the amount of energy . . .
flowing into my body. I will try and . . .
hold on . . . until we . . . arrive."

Max and the others turned to see Susan's
face contort into a ghastly expression. A
puff of smoke rose from her leg band and her
face suddenly went blank. She collapsed into
Max's arms her expression never changing.

"Susan! Susan! Talk to me please," Max
begged. They had arrived and Max ripped the
wires from her leg. He covered her body back
up as best he could.

"Something overloaded her systems," Mead
said.

-170-

"But what? The machine was functioning properly before we left," Max looked at Mead concerned.

"Remember when we first met? It was in the basement near the machine. Well before you came we saw Betsey come out of the machine. We thought she had been trying to communicate with the Represser."

"Instead, she wanted to destroy Susan," James said coming up next to Mead.

"It would appear so," Mead said.

"Well we still have a mission to complete, though if we don't find a way to fix Susan then it's a one way trip for us all," Max said sternly.

"The outside is clear LT., there's just piles of destroyed robots or somethin. We ain't been made yet," Tinker said from the door.

"Ok, Susan had said that we were located in a power conduit room. She said the main power reactor was in the next room to the right. Tinker, you and Bill set the charges. Mead, James go with them and provide cover fire if necessary. Povlov you and I are going to try and fix Susan," Max said looking into Povlov's eyes, He just nodded.

The four of them left the machine carrying the cases of explosives. Povlov looked over the computer console that was still active running off of Susan's energy. He tried using the keyboard to access Susan's memory banks only to find out that there were system failures throughout.

Povlov glanced up at Max and shook his head.

The Time Dominators

Betsey walked down the dark corridor to the room where the Represser was, the damage to her systems repaired. The Represser had accessed her memory banks to interpolate the information she had gathered. He now called for her to be at his side. He would probably give her a new mission. The door slid open and she entered.

The Represser stood in front of a large circular pad. On the pad were forty Annihilators, the green light grew from the center and moments later they disappeared. The Represser turned and looked down at Betsey.

"You have failed me miserably. You were to monitor their actions only! You disobeyed my direct programming not to harm Susan, now we only know that they will soon be coming," The Represser boomed.

He reached out and grabbed Betsey by the arm. His other hand swung out smashing against her face. He knew she felt no pain but the action seemed appropriate to him. Locking his hand around her throat he sent a surge of energy into her body shocking both her human and mechanical forms. This he knew she would feel.

Betsey fell back onto the floor her human face bruised and her arms and legs twitching from the power surge.

"You will not disobey me again!" The Represser boomed.

"Yes master, I will not fail you. My programing was over run by the absorbed emotions of the real human female," Betsey spoke with a mechanically synthesize voice that wasn't her own.

The Time Dominators

"It is the only flaw from the absorption
process. Even I am plagued with them. But it
is necessary for our complete resemblance of a
human. Without the emotions we would be
detected. You will be spared this time. You
are to use the scanners and detect were and
when they arrive, then destroy them all.
Fail me again and you will be erased."
    Betsey nodded and rose to her feet heading
for the doorway. She had to get to the scanning module, she would not fail her master
again.
    Tinker and Bill entered the main power
reactor room followed by James and Mead. The
room was immense with a cathedral ceiling that
seemed to go as far as the eye could see. In
the middle of the room sat a massive cube.
From the top and sides ran conduit power pipes
like they had seen in the next room. Colored
lights flashed on and off in sequence from
each side.
    Running up the middle all the way to the
roof ran a large black rod. They moved closer
to the cube feeling its pulsating power.
    "What do you think that large rod in the
center is used for?" Bill asked Tinker.
    "I don't know," Tinker replied.
    "The only way to find out is to follow it
up to the roof," Mead cut in.
    Bill moved forward handing his sniper rifle
to Tinker and taking his M16. He grabbed one
case of explosives by its roped handle and
headed for the ladder to begin his arduous
climb to the top.
    "Careful ole buddy," Tinker called to him.
    Bill just nodded and kept climbing. Tinker
started opening the crates full of plastic

explosive. He walked around the power unit
surveying it. He needed to place the charges
exactly right for the maximum effect. Mead
and James stood poised for an attack that
could come at any moment.

Every so often James looked up to see how
far Bill had gotten. Bill's pace was steady
as he climbed the steel rungs leading to the
top. His breathing became laborious and his
arm ached from the weight of the explosives.
He was almost there when he stopped and looked
down. Everyone looked like ants moving around
the power unit. Up ahead he could see an
opening where the ladder ended. There was an
uneasy darkness beyond it.

When he reached the top rung he peered out.
He could see buildings all level with one
another and all grayish in color. Beyond the
buildings where sand dunes. The sky was a
vermilion with purple streaks. Lightning was
constant and intense. He pushed the crate
through along with his rifle. Squeezing
through the small opening he found himself on
the roof. He grabbed his rifle and flipped
the safety off.

The buildings roof top was much higher
than the rest, in the middle of the roof sat a
colossal satellite dish. Every so often there
came a flash that caused Bill to cover his
eyes. Lightning struck the dishes center and
the power was absorbed and channeled downward
to the power reactor. Bill watched the
lightning strike a few times then poked his
head through the opening yelling down to the
others.

"It's hooked up to a satellite dish!" He
screamed.

"Blow it," Tinker screamed back up to him not stopping to look up.

"They must use the lightning energy to power the reactor, their feeding off the planet itself. They create conditions for the earth to produce lightning then harness it." Mead said looking at James.

"Incredible, unlimited power!" James said looking out the door.

From the scanning unit Betsey sent pulses over the whole complex. The impulses she received back showed humans in the main power reactor room and the next room. How long they had been there she couldn't tell. She relayed the information to the Represser who sent thousands of robot drones and Annihilators to the reactor section of the complex.

The Represser watched more of his Annihilators disappear on the glowing time pad. Nothing would stop his plans for total time domination. The humans would be destroyed and the threat would be over.

Tinker finished placing the charges and wired the timer. Nothing could stop it now, and if they tried to remove it or cut the wires then it would automatically blow. He stared up at the ceiling hoping to see Bill.

"Bill ya ox, where are ya!" Tinker called up.

Bill heard Tinker call, he had just finished setting his charges and he moved to the opening to head back towards the others. He didn't hear the clanking of metal on the roof top coming near him. There suddenly came a pulse of light different from the lightning flashes. Before he could react the light beam struck his leg severing it at the knee.

Bill howled in pain and collapsed on the roof top. He looked up seeing his attacker, a little girl he thought "No more than ten years old."

In the girl's hands was a rifle. It looked awkward in the child's hands because of its size. Another beam of light shot out grazing his arm. Bill again screamed in pain.

Down below they heard Bill's first cry. Tinker looked up his pulse racing. When they heard the second, Tinker moved to the ladder and began climbing. Mead grabbed him hauling back off the ladder.

"Get your damn hands off me ya bastard! That's my friend up there and he needs me!" Tinker yelled at Mead.

"Forget him, he's probably dead by now! They'll soon be coming in here!" Mead shouted.

Tinker looked up the ladder the need to go after his friend tearing him apart bringing back old memories of Nam.

Bill couldn't believe what he was seeing. The blood ran from his severed leg soaking the roof top. He pulled up the M16 and rattled off the clip into the child. The bullets pounded into the girl's chest ripping up the fleshy outer layer. Bill cried in anguish at what he was doing as the girl's blood mixed with his own on the roof top. The girl tumbled back off her feet.

Bill loaded another clip and watched the girl lay there for a moment then rose up, her form torn from the bullets.

"God forgive me!" He screamed, letting off another burst of fire from the M16. The

bullets tore into the girl knocking her back
down again the gun falling from her hand.

Bill dropped his gun and tried to stop the
bleeding from his severed leg. He felt faint
as he tied the makeshift tourniquet. Suddenly
he was slammed back down on his back. His
eye's opened in horror. The little girl stood
above him her foot planted firmly on his chest
not allowing him to get up. Her body was all
ripped apart and bloodied but she looked down
at him her face still intact.

She held up the rifle pressing the barrel
solidly between his eye's. Bill cried out, the
last thing he saw was a brilliant flash of
light then nothing.

Tinker heard him cry out then saw the flash
of light from the open hole. He looked at
Mead anger flaring in his eyes.

"If you hadn't stopped me I'd be up there
already!" He yelled.

"Look!" James yelled pointing to the
opening in the roof.

Something was coming through the hole. Its
form struggled to clear the opening.

"Bill is that you buddy?" Tinker yelled
out.

The form seemed to trip and abruptly fell.
Tinker yelled as he watched the form fall
towards them. James covered his eye's as the
body hit spraying blood everywhere. Tinker
rushed up to the body and rolled it over. He
turned in disgust. The head was completely
blown off, the torn flesh at the neck showing
burn marks.

"It was a beam rifle similar to my own."
Mead said callously over Tinker's shoulder.

Tinker looked up at the opening. He saw

the tiny form of what he thought might be a
child. He raised the sniper rifle with the
scope and viewed the face close up. It was a
child, a girl.

"It's a god damn kid," Tinker mouthed.

"You can't shoot, Tinker it's just a kid!"
James said stepping forward.

Tinker let the round off the sound of the
gun echoing in the room.

"It ain't no different than the Nam. The
kids are just as dangerous as the grown ups,"
Tinker said angered.

The bullet went through the opening
striking the girl in the head exploding on
impact. They shielded themselves from the
blast, as the debris fell from the ceiling.
James looked up, there was a gaping hole where
the opening had been. All around their feet
were pieces of concrete and metal parts
including blotches of blood.

James walked over and picked up a Locke of
bloody blond hair. He thought about his war,
there had been a definite enemy. Somebody
directly to vent the anger on. Tinkers war
was different, the enemy was unknown and came
in many different forms — including children.

From inside the machine Max heard the
rifle. He moved quickly to the door peering
out. Povlov moved quickly next to him.

"The others must have been detected," Max
said looking at Povlov.

Povlov nodded and looked back at Susan.
Her knees jerked and moved slightly. Then her
arms, Max could only hope that somehow she was
alive. Povlov tapped his arm. In the
distance the sound of metal against metal grew
louder. The others had not returned yet.

Max couldn't allow the others to be
separated. He rushed to Susan's side and
crouching down on his hands and knees.
"Susan, can you hear me?" He yelled.
Susan's head jerked up and down in a short
motion.
"Susan, can you still run the machine?" Max
asked.
Susan jerked her head sideways, then up and
down. She then jerked it up and down again.
Max exposed her leg band and looked at the
wires that needed to be inserted.
"Susan I don't know which wires go where,
you have to help me," Max said worried.
Susan's finger jerked out pointing to the
brown wire he had in his hand. Max took it
and inserted it into the top hole in the band
hoping it was right. She then began to point
to each successive wire. Max inserted them
counter clockwise. He looked at Susan for
approval seeing her head jerk up and down.
In back Max heard the clanking metal
drawing closer. He looked at the computer
screen to see them being activated by Susan.
Slowly time sequences began to come up on the
screen. She was preparing as best she could.
Now it was only a matter of time, the others
had to return before the Annihilators
prevented their escape.
Max grabbed the grenade launcher and
headed out to get the others.
"I've got to go and get the others! Stay
here and guard the ship," Povlov nodded and
poised his gun ready for the first Annihilator
that would come through the door. Max stepped
from the machine just as the first Annihilator
came through the door. Povlov's gun burst out

a beam of light striking the Annihilator in
the head disintegrate it in a splatter of
blood and metal parts.

Max stepped into the room calling Tinkers
name.

"We're comin LT., don't let the chopper
leave without us!" Tinker yelled as they moved
to meet Max at the doorway. Max saw Mead in
front heading towards him. Mead stopped and
raised his rifle pointing it at Max.

"What the hell?" Max yelled and dove to the
floor just as Mead fired. The beam of light
shot over Max into an Annihilator that had
come up behind him.

The Annihilator staggered back as the beam
struck its chest burning a hole in it. Behind
him were four more all advancing despite the
first one that fell. Max brought the grenade
launcher up and fired it. The explosion
ripped the Annihilators to pieces showering
the walls with blood. Max uncovered his head,
he lay amongst a pile of moving limbs and
parts.

"Are you hit Max?" James asked running up
to him.

Max looked down at his body, it was covered
in blood.

"I don't think so James. We have to get
out of here now! Susan's powering up the
machine as best she can," Max said.

"Your damn right we have to move, we have
two minutes before that thing in
there blows!" Tinker yelled.

They all rushed from the reactor room to
where the machine was. More Annihilators
poured in through the doorway. Others filled
the reactor room. Mead and Tinker both fired

hitting an Annihilator burning one exploding the other. Beams of light shot over their heads as they ran to the machine.

Mead watched Povlov shooting from the doorway. Moments later they were all in the machine.

"Susan now!" Max screamed.

In the reactor room an Annihilator looked over the explosives that were set and relayed the information back to the Represser. It then reached down and picked up the connecting wires disjoining one from the timer.

The time machine began to disappear when the explosion rocked the building. The concussion buffeted the machine. The control panel shorted and sparked, everyone was tossed from side to side. Susan screamed as her leg band sparked and shorted. Then the lights went out.

CHAPTER SIXTEEN

Mirage

Max awoke choking, the air was hot and
stifling and it parched his mouth. He was
laying on top of Susan who was pressed up
against the console. The whole machine was on
its side and everyone had tumbled into heaps
strewn about the insides. Povlov and Tinker
stirred from their resting spots against the
wall. Max tried focusing his eye's, his head
pounded and his body ached. James lay across
the chair in the middle, a nasty gash across
his forehead dripped blood slowly onto the
floor. Mead was awake, he moved over towards
Max.

"Where the hell are we?" Max croaked.

"It seems were someplace in the desert,
what time period? Your guess is as good as
mine," Mead said pointing to the sand blowing
into the open doorway.

Max rose to his feet wobbling, he made his
way over to James and felt for a pulse. It
was strong and steady. Max pulled him off the
chair and laid him down on the floor. He
reached below the seat where he had a small

first aid kit. He dressed and tended to
James's head wound, Mead helping him.
   Max then went over to Susan. Her blank
expression was one of pain. She stared at the
opposite wall oblivious to everything.
   "Susan, can you hear me Susan?" Max asked,
there was no response.
   "Susan please give me a sign, any sign
please Susan, move!" Max's voice became
desperate.
   Susan didn't flinch, her stare never
faltered. She still was connected to the
machine her leg band showing burn marks where
the power surge had shorted her out.
   "You gave your life to save us Susan, It
won't be forgotten," Max said softly.
   "What the hell are you talking about? It's
just a machine, it served its purpose," Mead
snapped.
   Max rose quickly grabbing Mead by his
body armor and slammed him up against the
wall.
   "You won't ever say that about Susan again!
 Do you hear me? You do and I'll kill you
myself! She's more of a human being than you
could ever dream of being!" Max yelled at
Mead no more than two inches from his face.
   Mead said nothing, he looked over Max's
shoulder at Povlov for reassurance. Povlov
turned his head avoiding Mead. Max let Mead
go and went back over towards Susan. He
grabbed the wires that hooked up to her leg
and began removing them.
   "Hey LT. look!" Tinker pointed to the
computer screen.
   The screen faded and the faint image of
their current date and time appeared then

faded away.
   "If that's right LT., then we just went
four hours into the past," Tinker commented.
   Povlov motioned with his hands an
explosion, then the time machine being hurled
away from the blast. Max watched him and
nodded. During their time displacement, the
blast must have forced them sideways in time
moving them to another location.
   Mead crawled his way out of the machine.
There were sand dunes as far as the eye could
see. He turned around and looked over the
machine in the opposite direction. In the
distance he could see the Represser's city.
The buildings looking ominous against the
hideous skyline.
   To the right about a mile or two stood
large rocky buttes rising out of the sand. He
looked at the sky, the purple streaks
contrasted greatly to the vermilion sky. The
lightning flashes were constant and he watched
them continually strike the largest building
in the middle of the city. Soon Tinkers
friend Bill would loose his life on top of
that building. Mead slid back inside the
machine.
   "We're about five Kilometers out from the
city which is in that direction," Mead said
pointing in direction of the city.
   "There are some rocky butts in that
direction, a kilometer or two away. I
think we should try and get to it maybe find
some shelter, this thing will soon turn into
an oven," Mead suggested.
   "He's right LT., its just like the Nam we
don't stay with the down chopper if we want to
live, they'll find us to easy," Tinker added.

"Ok, get as much gear and weapons at we can carry. I'll try and find some food or water."

Max opened the panel under the console. All he found were some bundled up clothes. He grabbed them hearing a clinking noise. Slowly he pulled them apart. Wrapped in the clothing were three bottles of champagne. His father must have stored them there for a celebration after his first time trip, only he never used them.

"Thank you Dad, your forgetfulness may just have saved our lives," Max thought to himself.

Max grabbed the clothing and began tearing it into large pieces. Taking a piece of cloth he wrapped his head with it letting the rest drape down over his neck. He then handed everyone a piece.

Mead picked up his beam rifle and looked at the bent tube barrel. He tossed it to the side and picked up James's grenade launcher and spare belt. The weapon was archaic to him but it would have to do.

Povlov grabbed his rifle and headed up out of the ship, Mead followed. They stood on top of a small dune looking at the skyline.

"Well my friend, here's where we find out what happened to all the others that escaped into the desert," Mead said.

Povlov looked over at Mead a disconcerting worried expression on his face. Mead understood, he felt the same way — afraid.

Tinker grabbed one of the champagne bottles and the sniper rifle crawling his way out of the ship. Max grabbed James and slid him up through the doorway to Tinker's waiting arms.

The Time Dominators

"You comin LT.?" Tinker called to him.

"I'll be up in a minute," Max said back to him.

He walked over and knelt down next to Susan. He picked her up, resting her head in his lap her expression never changing. Reaching out he brushed the hair from her face.

"I'm sorry for ever getting you into this mess. There's so much I wanted to tell you. Like how special you are and how much you really mean to me. Now I'll never get the chance. Rest in peace – my love – your sacrifice will not have been in vain, nor will your death. The Represser will pay for this."

Max finished removing the wires from her leg band. He dressed her covering her naked body. He then laid her down, reaching out he closed her eye's finally accepting her death. Grabbing the two bottles of champagne, the firstaid kit the grenade launcher and his sword he clambered his way up through the doorway.

He looked around, saying nothing he began to walk in the direction of the buttes, the others followed, Povlov carrying James. Max looked back at the machine, he couldn't say anything even if he wanted to, he was to choked up.

The going was slow, the sand hard to walk in. The heat was unbearable and their skin began to burn even though their clothes. Each one of them took turns carrying James.

The sky never changed, it's hideous color mixed and changed the color of everything else. They stopped at the top of a large

dune, allowing Max a few minutes to change
James head dressing. The bleeding had finally
stopped and James moaned a little then was
quiet. They shared a bottle of champagne
taking small amounts rationing the rest. Max
picked up James and they continued. They had
walked for three hours, the butte getting no
closer in the distance.

"What's goin on here, that thing should be
gettin closer to us by now," Tinker said with
a horsed throat.

"I don't know maybe it's some sort of
mirage," Mead said.

"I don't think so, it rises to high above
the sand. I think the heat rising off the
sand just made it appear closer than what it
actually was. Lets keep moving, by the way
the sky is darkening it will be night soon,"
Max said looking up at the darkening sky.

They trudged on through the sand each step
they took becoming laborious. Tinker was the
first to drop, his legs buckling out from
under him. Max rested James on the sand.

"I can't . . . seem . . . to control my
legs," Tinker said licking his dry chapped
lips.

"It was stupid to bring an invalid on this
mission and you know it!" Mead screamed at
Max.

Max lost all self control, he dropped his
sword and gun and launched himself at Mead
striking him firmly across the face. Mead
tumbled backwards into the sand. Max was on
him before he had time to get up. The two
tumbled wildly their fists striking each
other, their anger flaring. Suddenly a loud
crack filled the air. Tinker had discharged

his rifle.

"Stop it both of you, we have to survive. Save the fighting for the Represser! All of you go on, leave me here you don't need any excess baggage," Tinker said flopping back on the sand.

Povlov moved forward and picked Tinker up off the sand carrying him and his gun. He headed in the direction of the butte. Max looked at Mead the hatred clear in his eye's. Max picked up James and followed leaving Mead standing there. Mead shook his head and followed.

They hadn't moved more than twenty paces when the ground shook. Everyone stopped and looked in the direction of the city. The satellite dish on top of the reactor building exploded clearing off a large section of the roof. Then the whole building exploded a large billow of smoke rising into the air. Then the whole city began to detonate exploding into millions of fragments. The sky filled with smoke and debris. Across the horizon, they watched large spewing columns of smoke rise from other cities.

"Oh shit!" Mead screamed.

"I told you not to worry, when ole Tinker sets somethin to blow, it blows," Tinker said proudly smiling at Povlov.

A shrill filled the air and everyone looked around trying to find the source of the noise.

"There! Look!" Mead pointed.

Fifty feet in front of them a huge piece of concrete debris came flying down from the sky impacting in the sand and creating a massive creator. Sand sprayed high into the air covering them all. Then the sky began raining down debris from the size of pebbles to small houses.

"Lets get the hell out of here!" Max yelled running as fast as he could still carrying James.

The others followed, fragments hitting them causing welts from the impact. The butte lay just a few meters away. From a distance Max could see an opening at the base. Max and Povlov made it safely into the cave with Tinker and James. They watched Mead running for his life as the rubble crashed to the ground. Suddenly a large chunk struck the ground behind Mead. The impact caused Mead to be thrown into the air. He hit the sand and didn't get up. Max raced from the protective cover his body pelted from falling debris. He picked up Mead and headed back towards the cave.

"Come on, hurry! Hurry!" Tinker yelled.

Max made it back to the cave resting Mead up against the wall.

"Why . . . (pant) did you come after me?" He asked exhausted.

"Because I value life a lot more than you. I've seen enough death to last me a lifetime," Max said turning his attention towards James.

The jolting motion of running caused his head wound to open up again. Max redressed it looking at the limited supplies in the first aid kit. Povlov passed around the second bottle of champagne and they all took large swallows. Max poured some across James lips and he swallowed it.

"Well we're here so what do we do now? The Represser's destroyed, his plans thwarted.

How do we get home?" Tinker asked.

"Under different circumstances we could use our communicators and contact the others that are now orbiting the planet," Mead said looking out the cave entrance.

"In what time period?" Max said looking up.

He knew that Meads ship was in a totally different time period. His people had no idea that he was coming to this century.

"Even if they were here, our communicators wouldn't work in all the electrostatic emissions the atmosphere is putting out," Mead said looking skyward at all the rubble that showered down.

Through the cave walls they could feel the impact of the larger pieces as they struck the butte.

"This stuff could be coming down for hours. All that debris from every city got sucked up into the atmosphere. The stuff is tumbling around up there and is eventually coming down somewhere else," Mead said.

"What are our chances of getting home?" Tinker asked.

He looked at Max who just shook his head. They were now trapped here for the rest of their lives.

The Time Dominators

CHAPTER SEVENTEEN

Then There Were Three

From inside the time machine the
clinking of debris could be heard. But the
sound fell on deaf ears. Susan's body lay
next to the console her functions all but
terminated. Just outside the doorway the sand
moved, shifted from side to side. Then slowly
a two fingered hand emerged from the sand
followed by an arm. The head and shoulders
appeared. The head had no hair, the eyes were
large, black and positioned on the sides of
the head similar to a shark. The nose was
nonexistent and the jaw curved down showing
rows of sharp jagged teeth. The neck merged
into the huge powerful shoulders. The legs
were identical to the arms large and muscular.
The feet were shaped like the hands with just
two toes. The whole body was covered with a
thick outer shell like an armadillo.
    The creature moved forward into the machine
it's mouth dripping saliva. Its breathing was
steady and loud and it walked with a shifting
motion from side to side.
    It looked around the insides and then

-191-

spotted Susan laying silent and still. The
creature moved up next to her bending over
examining her. It reached its hand out and
gently touched Susan's skin feeling its
softness. It then touched its own. Looking
up it emitted a loud growl more of pain than
anger. It reached down and scooped up Susan
and headed for the doorway. It quickly
disappeared in the sand along with Susan
leaving the time machine totally empty.

Tinker rose to his mechanical feet and
walked over to Mead.

"Are you all right?" Max asked concerned.

"I feel a whole lot better now LT., I'll be
fine," Tinker said.

"We need to survive. That means we need to
find food and water. This cave can provide
temporary shelter," Max slapped the rock wall.

Max looked at the back of the cave, it
seemed to go on for quite some distance. He
took off his leather coat, the same one that
Betsey had worn. Removing his shirt and the
cloth scarf he made for his head he searched
around the cave for anything that looked like
a stick. Finding nothing he pulled his sword
out and wrapped the clothing around the end of
the blade. He patted his pants and jacket for
matches finding none.

"Does anyone have something I can light
this with?" Max asked.

Tinker walked over and produced a lighter.
Flicking the lid up and striking the flint the
flame shot up.

"It helps to light them fuses LT," Tinker
smiled.

"I'm going to explore the cave, there may
be more back here than we know," Max said

moving towards the back of the cave.

"Stay here, I'll be back as soon as possible."

Povlov rose to his feet and grabbed Max by the shoulder. He tapped his chest and pointed to the back of the cave. Max understood that he wanted to go, he nodded and smiled. They headed into the back caverns. The torch they made lighting up the way. The path was clearly cut and a foot trail clearly worn.

"But by what?" Max thought to himself.

The rock tunnel gently sloped downwards. They walked through a small opening, the tunnel then opened up into a large cavern. Max held the torch over the side in an attempt to see what loomed in the darkness. To the right of them the path dropped off into a dark oblivion, to the left a sheer rock wall.

The path gently became even steeper, Max turned and looked at Povlov who stood with his rifle ready to fire. He understood that Povlov expected to be attacked.

Mead watched the debris continue to fall. Tinker tended to James who was slowly coming around, he was incoherent still lapsing in and out of conciseness. Mead turned and headed back towards Tinker.

"How is he?" Mead asked.

"He should be in a hospital, that gash on his head sur looks nasty," Tinker said.

"We should have left him back at the ship, we'll never survive if we have to carry wounded around everywhere," Mead said looking disgusted.

"Just like me, huh bub. Why did you even come down to this forsaken place? To fight fer the human race? You've got to be kiddin,

scum like you have no idea what it's like ta
be human. Buddy you lost your humanity
somewhere's," Tinker nastily said to Mead.

"What right do you have to call me
nonhuman? We're fighting a war! We fight to
win no matter what the cost. We take the best
route open to us to succeed in our mission,"
Mead snapped.

"Buddy, you and your people have become
just like the machines your tryin to destroy,"
Tinker snarled.

Tinker's eyes grew wide as he looked beyond
Mead. A huge creature lumbered into the
caves' entrance. It's head was shaped like an
egg with large brown eyes and a monstrous jaw
showing many teeth. It didn't have ears or
hair. The body had four arms both with five
human fingers on each hand. The chest was
broad and thickly plated. The legs were
thinner than the rest of the body, the feet
were large and webbed. It made a croaking
noise like a frog and it pounded on its chest.
In back of it were others all different
and just as mutated. They all advanced into
the cave moving steadily towards Tinker, James
and Mead.

Mead brought the grenade launcher to bear.
Pressing the trigger, nothing happened. He
hit the side of it with his hand expecting to
fix it. Tinker grabbed it from his hands.

"What a time fer a damn dud!" He said
popping the useless grenade from the chamber.

Mead looked for a weapon, the sniper rifle
lay against the wall behind the grotesque
abomination that slowly came towards them.
There was no choice, Mead launched himself at
the creatures striking the first and knocking

him off balance. They toppled over onto the hard rock floor, the creature taking the brunt of the fall. Mead felt the four hands of his enemy grab him. He struck out against the creature with his fists succeeding in nothing.

He then reached down towards his left boot and grabbed a long slender knife. His wrist was quickly seized by the creature. Mead fought to bring the knife down towards the creatures throat but it overpowered him quickly compressing his wrist until he dropped the knife.

Tinker replaced the grenade and closed the launcher but it was too late. The other hoards of creatures stormed around Mead.

Before Tinker could pull the trigger the gun was ripped from his hands and smashed into fragments against the rock wall. Mead rolled off the creature in the direction of the sniper rifle. Before the creature could stop him Mead had grabbed the gun bringing it down and firing.

The boom was deafening in the small cave. The shell struck the creature in the abdomen hurling back against the wall then exploding in a shower of blood and parts. Another mutant with a large curled tail looking similar to a scorpion on two legs attacked Mead. It lashed out with its tail striking Mead in the hand leaving a deep bloodied welt.

Pain instantly shot up his arm causing him to double over. The creature grabbed the rifle and threw it to the other end of the cave. It grabbed Mead hoisting him into the air and throwing him against the rock wall. Mead collapsed in a heap.

The other creatures surrounded Tinker who backed up against a wall. None made aggressive moves towards him. Then one that looked like a cross between a human and a reptile pushed the others away. It stood in front of Tinker its one human eye looking him over.

Tinker could see his death happening in seconds. Moments later he was grabbed and forced down to the ground. He screamed as a multitude of different types of hands pressed him to the ground not allowing him to move.

Suddenly he felt his mechanical legs being torn from his frame. The wires connected to the box snapped shorting and sparking. Tinker watched in horror as the creatures held his mechanical legs studying them. One grabbed a leg from the other and smashed it against the wall making a gnarling sound. The other leg met the same fate. Tinker wondered if his arms were to be next. But they released him unharmed.

A mutation lumbered over and picked James up carrying him to the cave entrance, another grabbed Tinker by his shirt collar dragging him in the same direction.

"Mead! Wake up ya got to help us! Mead ya idiot, wake up!" Tinker screamed his arms outstretched towards Mead.

Mead stirred, his eye's opening barely but just enough to see James disappear into the sand with one of the creatures. Tinker's shrieks were silent to his ears which only heard a ringing noise. He wanted to do something but his body wouldn't move. He watched Tinker disappear below the sand also. They were leaving taking what they had come

for. Mead waited for his body to be jolted
into the air or dragged across the floor. The
darkness was slowly enveloping him, he tried
to fight it but quickly relaxed letting its
gentle calmness overtake. His last conscious
thought sent shivers through him.
    "In a barren desert where would you find
food?"

CHAPTER EIGHTEEN

Phoenix

The bang echoed throughout the cavern reverberating off the solid stone walls giving it no direction. Max and Povlov stopped dead in their tracks. The sound was definitely from a twentieth century gun.

"The others are in trouble!" Max bolted past Mead heading back towards the cave entrance.

Povlov could do nothing but follow. Max had left him standing in the blackness of the cave. He watched Max head up the trail the glow from the burning cloth creating an eerie bouncing ball. As long as he could see that orb he would know where to go.

Max had reached the small opening that lead to the larger cavern. He saw something crawl through the opening and lowered the torch so he could see better.

Mead looked up his face bruised and battered. He cradled his hand close to his chest the bloodied swollen appendage barely recognizable as a hand.

"What happened? Where's Tinker and James?"

Max blurted out.

"They took them . . . these mutant creatures. Hideous things, half human half insect or animal. There were dozens of them. They came out from under the sand. I got one of them but it looks as if they got me also," Mead said extending his hand.

Povlov had reached them, he saw Mead's hand and pulled a small container from the belt of his body armor. Max watched him working on Meads hand with first aid tools he had never seen. Povlov reduced the swelling and closed the open wound. Max wondered why Mead never did the same for James. Mead sat upright and exhaled feeling the pain from his wound subside.

"They just appeared from under the sand, I couldn't believe it! They could have gotten us anytime they wanted. I don't understand why they didn't take me though. Why just James and Tinker?" Mead shook his head.

"Well we can't just wait up there for them to come back. They probably won't either. I think our best bet is to head back down into the cavern. If they dragged them under ground then we might just find them down at the bottom of the cavern," Max looked down the trail into the darkness.

"We also need to find food and water, even just water right now would be nice," Mead said licking his lips.

"We may have a tough time of that. The Represser wasted this planet, the rain that comes down is pure acid. The human race started it back in the 1950's only to lead to this," Max shook his head in disgust.

"The old one's talk of the world being a

utopia, no suffering no disease and everything flourished," Mead said his throat raspy.

"Well it couldn't have been that much of a utopia, the Represser was build by your people and he's the one that devastated the planet," Max said bursting Meads impression of the old world.

Povlov helped Mead to his feet. Mead had dragged the sniper rile behind him, he wouldn't be caught without a weapon again. They headed down the path into the darkness. Max stopped to wrap another piece of cloth around the end of the sword. The light grew brighter and their field of vision increased.

They picked up their pace, Max in front, Mead in the middle and Povlov drawing up the rear. The trail began to get narrower until their backs were pressed up against the wall. Small stones were kicked off and they plummeted into the darkness below. They listened for them to hit but only silence greeted them. They pressed on, slowly the trail opening up allowing them to walk normally. Povlov stopped and listened, there was something behind them following. He strained his eye's to try and see something in the dark but found he couldn't.

Then he saw to his horror something that made him freeze in his tracks. Green eyes bounced up and down moving swiftly towards them. He tried to scream to the others but his throat only garbled faintly. They couldn't hear him, the glowing light from the burning cloth became distant.

Povlov turned to see the green eyes of the Annihilators almost upon him. He brought the beam rifle to hip level and began firing.

The cavern lit up as bright as daylight. The sudden change from total darkness to extreme light blinded them all. Povlov kept firing unable to see what he was aiming for. He knew the first volley struck its target. The flash of sparks and circuitry were clearly seen before the light blinded him.

Max and Mead turned and headed back towards Povlov. Their eyesight had been blinded but not as severely. For every flash that burst from the gun they could see hoards of Annihilators descending on Povlov. Mead brought the sniper rile up taking aim waiting for another flash of the beam rifle. When it came he fired hitting an Annihilator in the chest. The shell exploded and it toppled over the edge into the oblivion below.

Max rushed forward the flame from the sword flashing back and forth in the darkness. With each flash of light Mead fired the rifle taking out an Annihilator. He emptied the rifles clip. Tossing it down he rushed forward to enter the fray. Max's sword crackled with energy causing the blade to glow red.

He lashed out striking several Annihilators. They dropped in the pathway and were kicked over the edge by the others that advanced from the rear.

Max screamed. "We can't hold them back! Fall back down the pathway."

Through each beam of light that erupted from the rifle Max could see Povlov being overtaken. One grabbed him forcing the beam to shoot upwards hitting the cavern roof. They struggled back and forth, Povlov's hand

locked onto the trigger, the gun emitting a
solid beam upwards.

The cavern rumbled and shook. Max glanced
upwards to where the energy beam pounded into
the cavern roof. The beam had caused the roof
to split and it slowly began to crumble and
collapse.

Povlov felt his ribs being ground to dust
even through his body armor. His eyesight
slowly returned, he turned and looked at Max
who was moving forward to help him. He looked
over the Annihilators shoulder at the dozens
that were still advancing. Povlov took his
foot and pushed off the cavern wall forcing
them both off balance.

They toppled over the edge the beam of
energy still firing striking the walls
as they tumbled into the darkness. Povlov
felt his ribs give through the armor. The
darkness closed in around him, his last living
thought was that he had at least given his
comrades a chance. He couldn't allow them to
risk their lives for him.

Max watched briefly as Povlov and the
Annihilator fell into the abyss. The rifle
had kept firing and it quickly disappeared
from sight.

"Good bye my friend. I will avenge your
death, you will be a hero in the eye's of the
people," Mead said softly from behind Max.

They turned and watched the Annihilators
advance. Turning they both raced down the
pathway. The burning cloth at the end of the
sword was almost out. Behind they could see
the green eyes of their pursuers.

"Look!" Mead pointed to the pathway up
ahead.

The Time Dominators

There was a small light glowing in the distance. The closer they came the bigger it grew. In the side of the wall was a doorway. The light was bright beyond it and they fought to adjust their eyesight.

"We don't have much choice Max, their right behind us!" Mead pointed to the green eyes in the distance.

Max nodded and they entered into the bright light. A door snapped shut and they were instantaneously forced off their feet hitting the roof.

"Its and elevator! We're rocketing downwards," Max screamed.

The elevator abruptly stopped slamming them into the floor. They both lay in a heap as the door opened.

Max looked up at the towering face of his father, the Represser.

Tinker gaged his lips full of sand. He felt hands grab his shoulders as his stomach convulsed in spasms.

"Its OK, old boy. I don't know where we are but were safe for now," Came the familiar voice of James.

"It's good ta see yer up and around," Tinker mouthed spitting out grains of sand.

Tinker looked around, they were in another cavern. The walls cast light into the cave from pulsating phosphorous deposits in the rock. Strewn around on the ground were suits similar to Meads and Povlov's. They looked as if they had been tore to shreds. Sitting up on rock ledges were belts containing various supplies like medical kits and survival cooking tools. At the other end of the cave

-203-

were weapons like Povlov and Mead carried.

Tinker dragged his body across the dirt floor towards the guns.

"What are you doing my boy?" James questioned him.

"I'm gonna get us some weapons," Tinker said as he dragged himself.

"But why?" James quickly questioned.

"Look at them clothes over there, what do ya think happined to those poor saps? I'll tell ya, they became an afternoon snack!"

"But its not what you think, they haven't harmed us," James pleaded with Tinker.

Tinker had almost reached the guns when the lumbering form of a mutant entered the cave. It had a long neck and a slender body. Its head was human shaped with a curved beak forming where the nose and mouth were. It raised its arms revealing large wings that folded out.

From its throat it produced a high shrilling wail. James covered his ears the sound being magnified ten fold in the small cave. Tinker watched the creature move blocking him from the weapons. It shuffled its wings motioning Tinker to move back to where James was. Tinker obeyed not taking his eyes off the creature. James rose and helped Tinker across the floor. They both watched the creature crouch down at the other end of the cave apparently keeping guard over them.

James leaned over and whispered to Tinker.

"I can't help but notice the distinct resemblance this one has to a buzzard. Others take on similar forms of other desert creatures."

"I don't care what form they are, I just

want to get the hell out of here," Tinker said
nervously.

"But they haven't harmed us Tinker, I don't
know why but they haven't," James said trying
to reassure himself.

"Well I still think that were gonna be
lunch. They can't eat metal, that's why they
ripped my new legs off!" Tinker said still
irritated.

James shrugged, he couldn't explain why
they had taken Tinkers legs away. He
only had a feeling that they wouldn't be
harmed. Another creature entered
the room resembling a mix between a coyote and
a fox. It carried two carved out stone bowls
filled with clean water. It walked over to
them and placed them on the ground. It then
backed away out of the caves only entrance.

Tinker grabbed a bowl and handed it to
James who drank it down quickly. Tinker
reached for the other bowl keeping an eye on
the buzzard in the corner. The water tasted
good as it quenched his parched throats. His
attention was diverted when he watched a few
of them enter the cave. Tinker then dropped
his bowl his eyes growing wide.

"My god!" James muttered.

Susan walked in smiling, she walked over
to them.

"They had told me more were found. Are you
well?" Susan asked placing a hand on James
shoulder.

"Were as good as can be lady. I thought
you were back at that blasted machine deader
than a door nail!" Tinker thumbed over his
shoulder not sure of what direction the
machine was in.

The Time Dominators

"It would appear that Betsey, an Annihilator you haven't been acquainted with tampered with the time machines energy storage unit. When we transported through time I was unable to control the ships power. I maintained the ships functions through my own power control units. But then when we transported back out of the twentyfifth century, the city exploded.

The shock blew us sideways in time landing us out in the desert hours before we had first arrived. The blast also temporarily shut down all my systems. I needed to reroute the energy and slowly bring my systems back on line. When I regained my sight function I discovered I had been brought here by these people," Susan explained.

"People? Yer callin those things people?" Tinker blurted out.

"Those things as you call them were once like us. They are what's left of all the failed missions to destroy the Represser. The ones that survived escaped into the desert," Susan spoke softly.

"But what happened to them?" James asked.

"The planet had been ravaged by the Annihilators leaving an extremely harsh environment. Over a period of years they evolved and adapted to the planets surface each taking an image or images of various animals and creatures that use to inhabit the deserts."

"You can communicate with them?" James asked surprised.

"It took my programing some time to assimilate the language. But now I can communicate with them some what. They

know you mean them no harm as they do you,"
Susan said looking over towards the mutants
that stood around watching them.
    "Mean us no harm! They ripped my legs off!"
Tinker blurted out.
    "They did that because they thought you
were an Annihilator. Their hate for them is
great. If they knew that I was a machine I
would have been destroyed. When we blew up
the cities they were going to storm in and
finish all the robots off. But then they
discovered something even more important.
    The Represser has reduced this planet to a
wasteland by not letting any water flow to the
surface. The oceans are still there but are
so full of pollutants that they are
uninhabitable. He has contained all the
potable water beneath the surface in vast
contained oceans.
    There is a means of bringing it to the
surface only it is guarded by many
Annihilators," Susan said again looking at
the mutated humans.
    "They need our help then?" James cut in.
Susan nodded and sat down on the floor in
front of Tinker. Her eye's searched his
looking for answers.
    "Max...is he...?" She couldn't get the word
out.
    "No, Max ain't dead not by a long shot.
But he thinks your are. Mead and Povlov ain't
either. When those things attacked us Max and
Povlov had gone in search of food and water.
Mead killed one, but it wouldn't explain why
they didn't take him along with us," Tinker
muttered.
    Susan breathed a sigh of relief, her

The Time Dominators

greatest fear hadn't happened, Max was still
alive somewhere and she would find him no
matter what it took.

"Are we safe here?" James asked.

"As safe as anyone would be with the
Annihilators still around. The Represser may
have been destroyed but his flock of
mechanical men still follow their masters
programing," Susan said her memory banks
drifting.

They might all have a haven for now but
eventually if the Annihilators weren't
destroyed then the terror might someday
return.

Max was yanked out of the elevator by the
Represser. Another grabbed Mead holding him
off the floor by his body armor.

"It is so good to see you son. You have
been away for far to long," The Represser
spoke his voice stern, denoting great power.

"Your not my father!" Max snapped.

"No, not totally. You on the other hand
have been a distinct thorn in my side. I
should have destroyed you and your mother the
moment I captured you both.

Instead, I let these foul emotions that
control your frail forms influence my actions.
As a result you and the others have succeeded
in destroying my world. You may have
destroyed my cities but that can be rebuilt
along with the hundreds of thousands of
Annihilators you destroyed with them.

I still control the life giving water that
could revitalize the planet. I also control
various outposts in other time periods.
Eventually we will rise again to dominate

first time then the universe. We will live indefinitely while you will only exist a few decades. You are like an insect that can swatted and squashed. I only need to find the rest of your ill fated group along with my companion, Susan.

It was a bad decision on my part to return to 1954 and destroy her and her father it would have been pleasant to have a human host for my companion," The Represser gloated.

"But you said the human Susan had been killed by my father," Max said concerned.

"Don't look so surprised Max Storm. Your father came to us with cells from the real Susan. That is how we built the computer for the time machine. He did decide to try and destroy us though, by blowing up some power conduit lines. We then went back in time to get the real Susan after he had already returned. Unfortunately they both resisted and were exterminated.

I must admit though that I would have thought you would attack me directly. My informer failed in his mission. Like all the others that I sent to the planet Comm they were suppose to attack me directly. They had programming that would allow them to destroy others of their own kind but only to complete the mission. Susan was the one factor I hadn't planned on. Her resistance to me and knowledge of where the reactor unit was made you succeed in destroying my world. Only she would have known that every city was linked from that reactor. Therefore her destruction will cause me no more problems."

Max looked over at Mead then at the Represser.

"Your suspicions were right Max Storm. The one you call Mead is my informant and an Annihilator."

Max reeled from what he learned. The man that had traveled and fought along side of him was a machine. It would have explained some of Meads actions like leaving James to die or his harshness towards Susan and leading him into the elevator which was a trap. Max felt betrayed, he felt alone and abandoned.

The others were probably killed by the mutant creatures. That would have explained why they didn't take Mead. It was obvious that the Represser had no idea that Susan was already dead.

He was the only one left now. He had to find some way of destroying the Represser, then maybe the rest of the human race would come and start over again. If he could succeed, his death would be a small price to pay. Max's eyes were diverted past the Represser, from one of two doorways Betsey strolled in.

The damage that had been done to her had been repaired. She smiled at Max and clung onto the Represser's arm.

"Away from me scrap! You have failed me again by allowing them to destroy the reactor."

The Represser's hand came up striking Betsey across the face. She sailed through the air forcibly hitting the far wall. She rose to her feet her expression one of hatred.

"Get out of sensor range or I will reduce you to molten slag," The Represser growled.

"What another unplanned problem?" Max

snarled. He didn't like a woman to be hit
even if she was a machine.
"No, not a problem just the emotions again.
For some of us they are harder to control than
others. You will soon find out as you will be
quickly absorbed," The Represser said waving
his hand.
Max was forcibly placed on a upright steel
table, his hands and feet were shackled. He
looked around the room, it was barren except
for a stainless steel table on which his sword
lay the scabbard next to it. The Represser
turned and headed to one of the doorways.
Betsey cringed as he walked by expecting to be
struck again. Mead followed the Represser
out of the room along with the rest of the
Annihilators leaving Betsey and Max alone.
She rose to her feet and walked over
towards Max her eye's glinting from the
light in the room. Max said nothing, he
didn't allow his eye's to even meet hers.
"Why do you hate me so Max Storm?" Betsey
asked.
Max turned to look her in the eyes.
"Because you are an Annihilator, a machine
that tried to kill my friends and I."
"I only followed my programing. I have no
hate for you just Susan, she has taken you
away from me. You would have been mine
forever, until she came. How can you love her
and not me? She is a machine also," Betsey
asked.
"Susan shows kindness, a love of life - all
life. That's something that you'll never
know," Max said turning his head again.
"What if I showed this love of life? Would
you love me then like you did once before?"

Betsey said her voice sounding impatient.

"Maybe." Max said turning back to look her in the eyes.

Betsey turned and walked over looking out each doorway. She then came back and grabbed a shackle that bound Max's right arm. With an ease that astounded him, she snapped the steel cuff. Moments later he was free. Max bounded for the table grabbing the sword.

"Now go, I will find my own way out I cannot help you out of this complex. The Represser will be watching me and if he finds out what I have done I will be deactivated."

Betsey watched Max leave the room. Her emotions were in control now and for the first time she felt fear.

Susan rose and walked over to the mutants that watched them impatiently. James could hear her mumbling something which caused the others to make noises and odd movements. She came back and looked down at Tinker.

"We are going into battle. They are ready to rise up and destroy the Annihilators. They are sorry for destroying your legs Tinker. They wish that there was some way to rebuild them but they have nothing," Susan said softly.

"Don't worry about it, I've been without em' fer a long time now. It ain't nothin I can't handle," Tinker reached up and patted her on the shoulder.

"We will be given weapons along with those that can carry them. James you will be with us. Tinker you will remain at the entrance to these caverns to protect our retreat," Susan spoke with authority.

"I don't like bein out of the ruckus,"

The Time Dominators

Tinker frowned.

"We need you to cover our backs Tinker, you will also be given a transmitter and the codes to operate it. You will call the rest of the human race back to earth," Susan smiled knowing Tinker liked that idea.

"That's somethin I can handle. Lay that radio on me and lets git packin," Tinker beamed.

Max moved quickly but steadily down the corridor. The sword held tightly in his hand and the scabbard slung over his back. He didn't have a clue as to where he was going all he knew was that now he had a fighting chance. He could possibly find a way to escape, but he would be forced to survive in the harsh desert above. He might even succeed in destroying the Represser and freeing the water. In that case he would be alive and alone, trapped on the planet with no way back to his own time.

The corridor was rounded like all the rest he had traveled through. Dull lights bordered each side supplying just enough light for him to see. He expected to be attacked at any moment. It wouldn't take them long to discover he was missing. He kept following the corridor meeting no opposition. In the distance he could see that it opened up to a large room. He moved quickly coming up to the tunnels end. The room opened up into a large room, it was round in shape with a metal grated catwalk going completely around it.

From the catwalk there were tunnels leading in every direction. Max looked down from the rail of the catwalk. He could hear water but couldn't see it, the sound soothing his tense nerves. His lips and tongue hungered for just a cup full. He looked up, the round tunnel went all the way to the surface. Max could make out a tiny red speck of the vermilion sky.

Then it dawned on him walloping him hard. What he was seeing was exactly what he remembered in his dream.

Just then he watched the Represser emerge from the opposite side of the tunnel. Annihilators filed in behind him moving around the catwalk. Max turned to retreat when he saw that more were coming down the tunnel behind him. He had no choice, he had to stand and fight. His anger built remembering the Represser's face when he struck down his mother. Then the silent form of Susan laying motionless inside the abandoned time machine. James whom he didn't want to come was now dead.

He had broken his promise to Martha who would be alone when no one returned. Max turned, his sword glowing a bright red and charged towards his attackers. The sword flashed slicing one completely in half. The body fell off the catwalk towards the water below. Beams of light shot out of their weapons striking the wall tearing huge sections of concrete out. Some grazed his arms and legs giving him instantaneous third degree burns.

Max's forward advance never faltered. He locked arms with the next Annihilator, struggling to get the sword free. His hatred raged causing the sword to glow even brighter. The energy from the blade seared through the attackers hands leaving bloodied stumps. Max knocked him over the railing and advanced farther.

"Kill him! He is but one man, a human man!" The Represser growled.

More Annihilators emerged from in back of the Represser making their way along the catwalk. Max seeing the numbers, climbed over the railing and launched himself across the void below at the Represser. He struck the railing grabbing hold. The Represser reached down and grabbed Max by his left shoulder hauling him over the railing.

"Prepare to die Max Storm!" The Represser gnarled.

Max felt his shoulder crack as the Represser's grip tightened. The pain was excruciating and Max could see spots forming before his eye's. Max brought the sword up severing the Represser's arm that held him. The mechanical hand still remained tight on his shoulder but its grip loosened a little.

The Represser lashed out with his good hand striking Max across the face. The impact sent Max sprawling onto the catwalk his face a bloodied mess. The Represser was on him again hauling him up off the catwalk by the throat. Max began to loose consciousness, he needed air.

In desperation he struck out at the Represser embedding the sword into his chest. The blood sprayed out covering Max, he gaged as it spurted into his face. The Represser dropped Max who struck the railing and fell over the edge carrying the Represser with him from the sheer momentum. The sword handle lodged itself into the metal grating of the catwalk and ripped itself from the

Represser chest as he fell over the side with
Max.

They disappeared into the darkness below.
Max waited for his body to impact with the
water. When it did he felt himself losing
consciousness. The Represser's hand was still
firmly locked onto his shoulder he felt the
water begin to pour down his throat. His
dream had come true and he would soon be
dead.

CHAPTER NINETEEN

End Game

Susan followed the mutated humans through the vast dark corridors of the underground caverns. Tinker rode piggyback on Susan and James clung tightly to the long belt around her waist. They couldn't see where they were going and had no idea where they were exactly. Susan could see everything clearly her eyesight switching to infra-red in the dark. The mutants she thought had similar vision adapted to the dark tunnels below.

They came to the end of the tunnel where a large hole gaped in the wall. Beyond were the dim lights of a corridor. The leader of them all was a large half human spider. It peered though the hole checking to see if any Annihilators waited beyond. It crawled through using its additional four legs as support. Standing for a moment it motioned for the others to follow.

Soon they all poured through except for Tinker. He remained on the inside of the tunnel wall waiting for a sign to call the other humans to earth. Armed with a beam

rifle he also would cover their retreat if
necessary. They moved silently down the
corridor meeting no opposition. The corridor
opened up into a large room, it was barren
except for a massive bay door that encompassed
the entire wall. They cautiously entered, the
tension clearly visible on James face. He
reached out and grabbed Susan by the arm.

"I don't like this Susan. It's too easy,
it feels like a trap," James whispered to
her.

Susan never got the words out. The large
bay door slid up spilling in hundreds of
Annihilators and drone robots. Pulse beams
shot thick and wild, some striking there
targets others the walls behind them. Blood
splattered on both sides coloring the floor
red. The leader of the mutants quickly
moved over towards Susan. It spoke in a
dialect that she could interpret, it sounded
to James like clicking noises. She grabbed
James by the wrist.

"We have to go now!" She yelled.

"W..what? Where are we gong?" James
quickly said.

"We have been instructed to follow the
corridor behind the Annihilators to the end
where we'll find the main water shaft. There
is a meshed particle beam that covers the
water. It allows things in but not out, if we
can destroy the beam the water will be forced
to the surface and once started the Represser
will not be able to stop it," She spoke while
they dashed along the edge of the room slipping through the bay door.

Three Annihilators rounded the corner
heading for the room as reinforcements. James

shot the beam rifle disintegrating the head of the one in front. The others instantly went into a defensive program lashing out at Susan and James. Susan brought the palm of her hand up striking one in the jaw snapping its head from the neck. Blood sprayed and the Annihilator stumbled back and forth and collapsed its arms and legs kicking and twitching as its program tried to compensate for the damage. The second Annihilator grabbed Susan pinning her arms to her sides. It lifted her off the floor compressing her frame in an attempt to crush her.

James moved swiftly up behind pressing the rifle barrel against the Annihilators head. It released its grip on Susan to deal with the new threat but it never had a chance. James pulled the trigger, the head disappeared and the body collapsed in a pool of blood on the floor.

"Thanks!" Susan smiled at James.

"No problem my dear. Just call on Sir James any . . . ,"

James words were cut short as a particle beam grazed his left shoulder. The force of the beam knocked him off his feet sliding him across the floor leaving a red streak. An Annihilator stood in the hallway gun poised ready to fire again. Susan only had a split second to make her move. She rolled to the floor as another beam shot out barely missing her. She rolled and slid kicking the Annihilator's feet from under him. The beam rifle shot wild ripping out sections of the corridor.

Susan was on the Annihilator before he could get back up. She struck him in the

chest driving her hand through his skin and
into the metal breast plate. Grabbing wires
and circuit boards she ripped them out in an
attempt to short his circuitry. The hole sparked
and shorted but the Annihilator kept moving.
Suddenly its head disappeared before her
eye's. She looked up expecting another
attack. Instead she found Mead standing there
bruised and battered but smiling. In his hand
he held his own beam rifle.
     "Looks like I got here just in time," Mead
said out of breath.
     "Get over here, help me see how bad James's
wound is," Susan said paying no attention to
Mead's first comment.
     James lay sprawled out on the floor a pool
of blood forming on the floor. Susan looked
at the wound, the beam had just grazed his
shoulder but cut a deep gash. The skin around
the cut had third degree burns. James stirred
rubbing his head with his good hand. He
winced when he tried to move his arm.
     "Looks like they got me Susan," James
smiled the pain clearly visible on his face.
     "Hang on, I'm going to get you out of
here," Susan began to pick him up.
     "Susan you have to go on, finish the job,"
James sternly said.
     "But your wounds, you . . . ," James cut her
short.
     "A lot of people died to get to this point.
You have to finish it or their sacrifice with
have been for nothing," He looked strait into
her eye's.
     Susan understood what he meant. She
reached down and helped him up against

the wall. James looked up past Susan.
"Susan look out!" James screamed.
Susan moved to the side but not quick
enough. A particle beam struck her shoulder
blade penetrating the synthetic skin and
destroying the circuit boards underneath.
Susan picked herself up her right arm useless.
Mead stood holding the beam rifle a grin
coming across his face.
"You really don't think I'd allow either of
you to reach the water shaft now do you?" He
began to laugh.
"But, I don't understand. Mead I thought
you were on our side," James blurted out.
"He's an Annihilator planted to make sure
that our mission failed," Susan looked at Mead
anger in her eye's.
"That is correct, I am an Annihilator. My
mission would have succeeded if it wasn't for
you Susan. I hadn't figured the possibility
that you knew where the main power reactor
was. You have a proverbial pain in the ass
since the beginning.
I was also sent to meet Betsey not destroy
her. According to my mission program we were
to destroy you all but Betsey violated her
programing."
Mead seemed to enjoy telling them how much
they had been deceived. Susan could tell that
his absorbed human emotions were now coming
out. If James could just distract him enough
she might be able to force him through the
tunnels entrance into the water shaft. After
that she didn't have a clue on how she was
going to defeat him with only one good arm.
"It didn't deceive me Mead, and you sure as
hell didn't deceive Max!" James shot out.

Anger brewed on Meads face.

"I am superior to vile human life! And I am clearly superior to a walking pile of gears," He said looking at Susan then back at James.

The moment had come and Susan launched herself at Mead. He never saw her coming, she struck him in the stomach knocking the beam rifle out of his hands. They both rolled back through the door into the water shaft. She struck out at Mead's left knee snapping it through the body armor. He collapsed onto the grating grabbing Susan's ankle.

Pulling himself closer to her he increased his grip trying to crush her ankle. Susan lashed out with her other free foot hitting Mead in the head repeatedly. The flesh on his face bruised, then bled and slowly began to peel off revealing the gray metal plating beneath. The eyes burst from the pressure uncovering the green mechanical orbs behind.

His advance never halted despite Susan's repeated blows. He crawled his way on top of her his face dripping blood. His teeth were clenched in satisfaction.

"Maybe this was the way I should have taken you before!" Mead snarled.

Susan felt trapped, her human cells cried out in an emotional pain that made her feel fear. She turned and looked for something to use as a weapon. Her eye's fell on something that made her heart sink even further.

Within an arms distance jammed into the grating was Max's sword. If Max had lost his sword then he might very well be dead and Mead most likely was the killer. Her fear was

quickly replaced with anger and she stretched
trying to reach the sword with her good arm.
Mead continued to crawl his way up her body
reaching for her throat.

"You'll never reach it bitch! Your pitiful
existence will soon be terminated," Mead
snarled again.

Susan felt that he might be right, but she
kept trying to reach the sword. She couldn't
give up hope she had to avenge Max's death.

"I must reach the sword!" She thought to
herself. Mead laughed his voice filling her
sound impute sensors creating a echo.

Instantaneously Susan felt a violent nudge
as Mead was ripped from her striking the
railing. She didn't hesitate, grabbing the
sword she rose to her feet poised ready. In
the tunnel entrance lay James sitting against
the wall unconscious a beam rifle sliding from
his hand. Mead rose up onto his good foot
using the railing as support.

"You better use it well whore, you won't
get a second chance. You are just a machine,
you will never be capable of human thoughts
and emotions! Your programing won't allow
it!" Mead taunted her.

Rage boiled inside Susan, a rage like
nothing she had ever felt before. Her
thoughts became blurred as her anger consumed
all. The sword began to glow a bright red its
energy crackling. Mead's jaw dropped as he
watched the sword glow.

"It can't be possible! Your not human!"
Mead screamed launching himself at Susan.

The blade sliced into Meads shoulder at the
neck and kept cutting until it came out at the
base of his opposite rib cage. The shocked

The Time Dominators

look still remained on his face even though
his body was now in two parts. Susan lowered
the sword feeling drained. She now knew the
truth about herself, she was a human locked
inside a computer chip.

Max felt the water rush down his throat,
the Represser's severed hand still locked on
his shoulder. Max began to resign himself to
oblivion when he felt hands grab onto his
jacket pulling him somewhere. Moments later
his lungs gasped air. He began hacking and
coughing, the water in his lungs coming up.
His strength slowly began coming back and
his eye's focused. Sitting in front of him was
Betsey her hair and clothes soaking wet. She
reached out and pried the hand from Max's
shoulder tossing it back into the black water.
They were on a large platform that opened up
to a large room. Max could make out in the
dim light that the walls were lined with
computers their lights flashing on and off.
He turned his attention back to Betsey.
"I don't understand, why did you save me?"
Max asked bewildered.
"I saved you because I love you Max Storm.
The Represser had promised me that you'd be my
companion. He has and lied to me, my
programing is exact and precise but my
absorbed human emotions are also very strong.
Those emotions are for you Max Storm," Betsey
said leaning over.
She gently placed her lips against his. Her
kiss was cold and deathlike, not like Susan's
that was warm and very much human. Max
continued to kiss Betsey, he didn't need
to fight Betsey along with the Represser. He

opened his eye's looking over her shoulder.

The Represser stood there holding a rifle.
Max grabbed Betsey trying to move out of the
way but it was to late. Betsey turned her
head just as the Represser fired. The beam
hit her square in the back the force from such
a close blow threw Betsey into Max and they
both tumbled across the grating. The
Represser fired again striking her in the hip.
Her leg bled profusely and it dangled back and
forth a thin piece of metal holding it
together.

She looked up at Max her eye's pleading with
him to help her understand. She reached up
and touched his face.

"Max Storm, you will remain in my memory
always. Understand that even machines can
learn to love," She never got to say anything
else.

Another blast from the Represser struck her
chest burning a large hole through the skin
and into the circuitry. Betsey's existence
terminated at that moment.

Max looked up at the Represser, he knew
that his death was next. The Represser
lowered the gun aiming right at Max's head.

"This is the end Max Storm but there is one
thing I wish to show you before you die," The
Represser looked to his right.

From out of the shadows stepped Virginia
Storm. Her wounds had been healed and Max
knew that she was an Annihilator. Fear gripped his body, he might have been able to
defeat the Represser but not both.

"You see, I had to construct another
companion since the one I made revolted and
attached herself to you. This one on the

other hand is more obedient. I did not give
her complete self awareness both mentally and
physically like I did Susan. Watch and you
will see," The Represser handed the beam
rifle to Virginia.

"Kill your son! Kill Max Storm!" The
Represser commanded pointing at Max.

Virginia raised the rifle aiming it at
Max.

"Mom, don't," Max said softly.

Virginia hesitated, "Kill him now!" The
Represser's voice boomed.

She took aim, Max closed his eye's waiting
for the end, there was no escape now. He
would be killed by the one person he wanted
most to save. He heard the beam shoot from
the gun and yelled.

He opened his eye's, Virginia Storm stood
pointing the gun in the opposite direction.
The Represser stood there his mouth open, a
large smoldering hole had been seared through
his chest. Max could see sparking wires and
broken circuit boards along with ripped
tissue.

"There is no way Sam that you can force me
to kill my own son," Virginia said softly.

Virginia fired again and kept firing the
hatred etched into her face. The Represser
took each hit forcing him back. His legs
buckled from beneath him and he collapsed on
the edge of the grating. He looked up at
Virginia his blood covered face still showing
surprise. Virginia walked up to him aiming
the gun directly at his head. His mouth
opened wider as if to say something, then he
was gone.

Max stood and watched his mother, she

walked over to him handing him the rifle.

"Not all the Represser's programing was correct. Max you must search out and find all the Annihilators and destroy them. Given time they would one day rise up rule the planet again. You must do this, for your fathers sake you must destroy the wheel he set in motion.

The major part has been done but in other time periods Annihilators still exist their programs still functioning. My time has come Maxwell, you must finish what has been started," Virginia raised the gun in Max's hand pressing it against her chest.

"I...I can't do it Mom, please don't make me do this. Come back with us, you can exist in our time period," Max pleaded.

"No Maxwell, at this moment I am barely controlling the Represser's programing. I can not hold it very much longer, you must do it or I will be forced to destroy you," Virginia said softly.

"I just can't do it, I can't" Max said the tears running down his face.

"You must and you will. I love you Maxwell," Virginia reached out and pushed Max's hand that was gripped on the trigger.

The beam burst through Virginia's chest ripping out her whole back. Max's scream echoed up the shaft. He stood there frozen and numb watching her body fall over the grating and into the water. The expression on her face never faltered and Max thought he almost saw her smile.

He collapsed to his knees, his grief consuming him. He just stared at the water not even hearing Susan's voice calling from above.

Susan found a way down to reach Max. She placed her hand on his shoulder. She had witness Virginia's destruction. Max turned and looked up at her. Susan smiled and Max rose to his feet holding her in his arms. There lips touched and their kiss was passionate.

"I thought you were dead," Max said his voice cracking.

"When I found your sword up above I thought you were also. I thought Mead had killed you," Susan said touching his face.

"Then you know that Mead was an Annihilator?" Max asked.

"Yes, he's also been destroyed," She motioned upwards with her eye's.

Susan looked down at the mauled form of the Represser. Then at Betsey's broken form.

"It's over now isn't it," Susan said.

"Not by a long shot, there are other Annihilators in other time periods. We have to destroy them all," Max said.

Susan nodded, she knew that he was right none of them would ever be safe until they were all found. Max and Susan walked into the room housing the computers. They still needed to turn off the particle field allowing the water to rise to the surface.

"Do you understand any of this?" Max asked.

"There's nothing in my memory banks, if you give me time I probably could figure out how to work it," Susan said touching the console.

"No time, move out of the way," Max motioned for her to move back.

He raised the particle beam gun and fired

at the console in rapid secession. The beams
blasted into the computers blowing pieces
everywhere. Susan shielded herself from the
debris. She turned and looked up the shaft to
see if the field was still on, she couldn't
tell.

In the room the circuitry sparked and
shorted then the lights went out. There came
a rushing sound from deep beneath their feet.
It slowly increased in intensity until they
had to hang onto each other for support.
The water began to churn, bubbles rising from
somewhere below escaped from the top.
Suddenly the water shot up the shaft creating
a huge column of. It ripped through the
grating tearing it to pieces carrying Meads
body with it. It burst out the top forming a
mountainous geyser.

James sat inside the tunnel, the force kept
the water in an upward motion keeping the side
tunnels dry. He watched in fascination, a few
mutants came carrying Tinker.

"Hey man is this great or what!" Tinker
yelped.

James patted him on the back smiling. They
sat there watching the water.

"All the rest of the human race is on its
way back to Earth. I kinda hated to stay out
of the ruckus. I knocked off a few of them
machines when they tried to escape," Tinker
praised himself.

"The returning people need to be informed
that there are Annihilators among them," James
said turning to Tinker.

Tinker nodded. "Has anyone see the LT. or
for that matter Susan? What about Mead and
Povlov?" Tinker asked.

"I haven't seen Max, I fear he's gone. Susan disappeared below just before the water shot up. Povlov's dead, Mead turned out to be an Annihilator," James explained not wanting to get into details.

"Doesn't surprise me none. The man wanted to leave us all to die," Tinker shook his head.

James looked back at Tinker when he saw Max and Susan emerge from the other end of the tunnel.

"Max! Thank god your alive!" James shouted. Tinker rolled around to face them.

"Good ta see ya LT.! I kinda figured no less from ya though," Tinker smiled.

"Well were all together again, the world has now been returned to the people. It's time for us to go home," Max smiled.

"The mutants give us their thanks and blessing. They will finish the cleanup. Our machine has been brought back to a cavern not far from here," Susan added.

"Are you going to be able to run it?" Max looked at her seriously.

"You've got to be kidding! I'd run that thing to get us out of here if I had to get out and push myself!"

They all began to laugh and headed back down the tunnel knowing that their job was done, at least for now.

Epilogue

The dull bonging of the grandfather clock brought Max back to his senses. Glancing up at it he noticed that he'd been reminiscing for almost two hours. The fire had burned itself down to a pile of glowing embers. Max stared at the newspaper clipping then closed the book.

"No, it's not over yet. There will be others," Max thought.

He was startled when a pair of soft hands slipped down over his shoulders. He looked up to see Susan's warm smiling face. She moved around and sat down in front of the fireplace. She wore a very sexy and very sheer nightgown that went all the way to her feet. Max looked at her very much aroused.

"Been thinking about what happened?" Susan asked, her voice sounding very soothing.

"Yeh, kind of, I begin to wonder if coming to the year 1992 was such a good idea," Max asked.

"Well we didn't have much choice, my time circuits were a little out of wack. Anyway we went back and brought Martha back, rebuilt the house and everything is fine now," Susan said as she grabbed the poker and stirred the coals, the fire slowly came back to life burning the pieces that still remained.

"Why don't you come down here with me and
we can talk about it in front of the fire,"
Susan said as she sprawled out keeping her
eye's on Max.

Max got up from his chair and knelt down
bringing his lips to hers passionately
kissing her. She sighed when he drew away.

"Remember a relationship takes time, and
your special enough to me to take that time,"
Max said smiling. He wanted nothing more than
to give in to her. But he wouldn't, Susan was
special and it was one thing he didn't want to
ruin. Max turned and left the room leaving
Susan sitting by the firelight. She placed
another piece of wood on the fire and watched
the flames rise.

"Someday Max Storm, Someday we'll be
together," Susan thought and watched the
flames dance back and forth.